THE **FORTUNES** OF **TEXAS**

SHIPMENT 1

SHIPMENT 2

SHIPMENT 3

SHIPMENT 4

SHIPMENT 5

Mendoza's Secret Fortune by Marie Ferrarella
The Taming of Delaney Fortune by Michelle Major
My Fair Fortune by Nancy Robards Thompson
Fortune's June Bride by Allison Leigh
Plain Jane and the Playboy by Marie Ferrarella
Valentine's Fortune by Allison Leigh

SHIPMENT 6

Triple Trouble by Lois Faye Dyer
Fortune's Woman by RaeAnne Thayne
A Fortune Wedding by Kristin Hardy
Her Good Fortune by Marie Ferrarella
A Tycoon in Texas by Crystal Green
In a Texas Minute by Stella Bagwell

SHIPMENT 7

Cowboy at Midnight by Ann Major
A Baby Changes Everything by Marie Ferrarella
In the Arms of the Law by Peggy Moreland
Lone Star Rancher by Laurie Paige
The Good Doctor by Karen Rose Smith
The Debutante by Elizabeth Bevarly

SHIPMENT 8

Keeping Her Safe by Myrna Mackenzie
The Law of Attraction by Kristi Gold
Once a Rebel by Sheri WhiteFeather
Military Man by Marie Ferrarella
Fortune's Legacy by Maureen Child
The Reckoning by Christie Ridgway

THE **FORTUNES** OF **TEXAS**

FORTUNE'S PROPOSAL

———— ⚹ ————

NEW YORK TIMES BESTSELLING AUTHOR

Allison Leigh

⬦ **HARLEQUIN**® THE FORTUNES OF TEXAS

Special thanks and acknowledgment are given to Allison Leigh for her contribution to the Fortunes of Texas: Lost...and Found miniseries.

Recycling programs for this product may not exist in your area.

ISBN-13: 978-1-335-68033-4

Fortune's Proposal

Copyright © 2011 by Harlequin Books S.A.

Printed in U.S.A.

Though her name is frequently on bestseller lists, **Allison Leigh**'s high point as a writer is hearing from readers that they laughed, cried or lost sleep while reading her books. She credits her family with great patience for the time she's parked at her computer, and for blessing her with the kind of love she wants her readers to share with the characters living in the pages of her books. Contact her at allisonleigh.com.

In loving memory of Larry

Chapter 1

"Happy New Year, Deanna. Hope you have fun tonight."

The farewell was echoed three times over as Deanna Gurney watched the last of her co-workers at Fortune Forecasting head out the office door.

She sighed faintly and looked at the round watch on her wrist.

It was nearly eight. Four more hours, and she could put the close on another year.

She sighed again and slowly tapped the end of her red pen on the surface of her desk as she stared blindly at the article she was supposed to be proofreading.

The tapping might as well have been a clock ticking.

A new year was supposed to be the start of new things, wasn't it?

Unfortunately, she couldn't help but think that the "new" was likely to turn out worse than the "old."

Depressed by her own thoughts, she shook her head and focused again on the article that her boss had decided just had to be completed before the office took their brief New Year break.

Trust Andrew Fortune not to realize that his latest burst of creative, financial genius was inconveniently timed when it came to the rest of his staff.

She corrected a spelling error and felt her gaze drifting upward to the opened doorway of her boss's office.

Drew wasn't sitting at his desk. If he had been, she would have had a straight-on view of him. Instead, she only caught the occasional glimpse of him as he paced around his spacious office, passing behind his desk occasionally to stop and look out the windows that offered a near-panoramic view of San Diego. During the day, she knew he'd be able to see all the way to the coastline.

Now the only thing he'd see out those windows was the night sky and city lights.

Even as she watched, he paced past the doorway, completely oblivious—as he had been for most of the day, since he'd spread the word that he wanted this last project done before they shut down for the long weekend—to anything that was transpiring beyond his office doorway.

He wore a Padres ball cap on his brown head, the bill pulled down low over his brow. A sure sign that his mood was just as dark as the grim set of his angular jaw suggested. When he was feeling particularly good-natured, that hat would have been turned backward with the bill scooting down his neck and there would have been a cocky half twist to his lips, a faint dimple in his right cheek and a wicked glint in his dark brown eyes. He'd have been holding a golf club in his hand, practicing his putting across the smooth, thick, beige carpet that lined his office instead of clenching the end of a baseball bat in his hand.

The faint buzzing of her cell phone drew her attention and she picked it up off the desk, looking at the display.

Gigi.

She sighed again and set the phone down, unanswered.

Her mother had already called her a half dozen times that day. Deanna had no desire to talk to her, yet again. Hard as it had been, she had already said what she'd had to say.

But the vibrating phone reminded her that she did have work to do that didn't involve lollygagging around, worrying about her boss's state of mind.

She had plenty of reason not to feel particularly celebratory. But Drew Fortune had the world by the tail. He was thirty-four years old—eight years older than she—and handsome as sin, plus he was poised to take the helm of the hugely successful trend analysis firm his father had founded decades earlier. And if not for the fact that she knew what his plans for that day were supposed to have been—flying to Texas—she was certain that he would have been heading out with one of his leggy, buxom blondes on his arm who'd have undoubtedly ensured that she rang in his new year in a major way.

Deanna made a face and scratched her red pen through a redundant phrase.

"Hell, Dee. That page looks like it's bleeding."

She didn't look up at her boss. "It's one of the things you pay me for, remember?" She corrected another misspelling.

Brilliant, he was. But a good speller?

Not exactly.

"Seems to me I'm also paying some other folks who ought to still be around." Drew sat on the corner of her desk and picked up her cell phone as if he had every right to do so. He tapped the end of his baseball bat against the toe of his leather shoe.

"We didn't need the rest of the staff here to finish up the article." Everyone had pulled together the data that he'd needed. The only thing left now was for her to finish proofing it, send it via email to their bazillion clients and then to the newspaper that was printing it in Saturday's New Year's Day edition.

He made a low sound that seemed distinctly displeased. "So you decided who stayed and who went?"

"Everyone stayed as long as they did because you asked them to," she said evenly. "But once their tasks were complete, did you really expect them to sit around and twiddle their thumbs until I finish my end of it?"

He grimaced.

"Besides, it's New Year's Eve," she reminded. "People had plans that didn't necessarily include hanging around here." Including him, because he was supposed to have been on the company jet hours ago.

He lost interest in the phone and picked up her stapler instead. "Did you have plans?"

She sighed, set down her red pen and folded her hands on top of the draft. "Yes, as a matter of fact."

"A date, I suppose." His dark, level brows were barely visible beneath his pulled-low cap. "What was his name? Mike?"

She kept her expression calm. It was easy enough. She'd had plenty of practice staying calm in the four years she'd worked for him. And before that, a lifetime of being Gigi's daughter. "It was Mark, actually." Which Drew knew very well because he'd met the man several times during the nine months she'd dated him. "And we broke up."

His brows pulled together. "Since when?"

Since my mother. The caustic answer leaped into her brain, but she held it back. The problems that she had with Gigi had nothing to do with her work. "A few months ago."

Drew's lips twisted. "Nothing like true love," he muttered. He set down her stapler and pushed off the desk. "So who is the date, then?"

She couldn't imagine what was spurring his sudden interest in her love life, but then she couldn't imagine what had put that hard, grim look on his face either, or this sudden, unusual…hovering…while she worked.

"Dates. Plural." She smiled slightly, wryly enjoying the novelty of the speculative look from him that she earned. "Three of my girlfriends," she added. "So stop looking so impressed. We're planning a spa weekend, as it happens."

Her phone vibrated again and she pressed a button, silencing it. "No men at all," she concluded. And no frantic calls from Gigi, she vowed silently.

Her mother had made it very clear that she'd expected her little Deedee to drop everything and come sit by her side in her latest hour of need, even if it was New Year's Eve. And she'd made it abundantly plain how she considered Deanna's refusal to do so an utter betrayal.

But then, Gigi was nothing if not melodramatic.

It didn't matter to her mother that Deanna had spent most of her life rearranging her life to accommodate Gigi's needs.

"Where at?"

"Up in La Jolla." She named the resort. "I was supposed to meet them two hours ago so we could all drive up together. Instead, I'll have to meet them there." She knew better than to expect Drew to apologize, though. That wasn't exactly his method. And it wasn't as if La Jolla was far. A handful of miles only.

It just was not what they'd planned.

And all because Drew was in a clearly bad temper.

He was pressing the end of the bat into the thick carpet, his expression still black, and she chewed the inside of her lip as she tried not to watch him.

But it was hard.

He was a man made to be watched. Thick brown hair that was usually just this side of rumpled—unless he had an important meeting and then he'd slick it back and look even more devastating. Wide shoulders and a lean build that looked just as good beneath his custom-made suits as they did when he was shirtless and entertaining clients on the beach.

Yes, Drew Fortune was certainly watchable.

But not touchable, her mind whispered.

She knew better than to mix business with pleasure. She'd learned that well simply by watching the messes that her mother made. That her mother was continuing to make.

Not that Deanna had to worry that Drew might think of her in that way anyway. She did her job and she did it well, and that was the only thing he cared about.

Which was exactly how she wanted it. Give her professional respect over a romantic dalliance every day of the week and twice on Sundays.

She enjoyed her work with Fortune Forecasting, and ordinarily, she liked working for Drew Fortune. And right now, given Gigi's latest exit from reality, Deanna needed the distraction of her work more than ever.

She picked up her pen and forced her attention back to the page. "I'll be done with this in ten minutes," she promised. "Then you can get out of here, too." So could she. She'd join her girlfriends and try to forget for a few days that her mother—still jobless since her last one ended in its usual emotional meltdown—was on the verge of financial ruin and blamed Deanna for not wanting to save her.

She couldn't understand at all that Deanna simply couldn't save her.

"Hallelujah," Drew was saying, his tone

flat, almost as if he were answering her own silent thoughts. "Just get the article done."

Her jaw tightened a little with annoyance. What did he think she was doing?

Once again, her cell phone softly buzzed against the surface of the desk and she opened the top drawer of her desk, tossed it inside and closed the drawer again.

She still imagined she could hear it silently vibrating against the collection of pens and paper clips inside.

"Why don't you just turn the damn thing off if you're not going to answer it?"

Good question. "She'd just start calling the office line, then."

He lifted the baseball bat and rested it over his shoulder. "She?"

"Gigi."

"Your mom must be pretty anxious to talk to you. Six calls from her at least."

Which he knew because he'd looked at her cell phone. "She's annoyed that I didn't include her in my little New Year's vacation." At the mammoth understatement, her pen nearly went right through the paper as she struck out another phrase. "Did you know that you repeated yourself twice here about the Decker rebound?"

He sat again on the edge of her desk and slid the paper out from beneath her pen. He glanced at it, then handed it back. "That's what I've got you for."

Misspellings were usual for him. Repetitive phrasing was not.

She quickly continued reading, but for some reason it was harder than it usually was ignoring the bulge of his very well-shaped thigh beneath his charcoal-gray trousers.

And there was at least a yard of space between them.

"I, um, I hope you're already packed for your trip to Texas." She realized she was skimming the last paragraph and made herself slow down. The last thing she wanted to do was disseminate something with an error that she should have caught just because she was feeling particularly distracted by her boss. "Because you're supposed to meet the jet at the airfield in two hours." She'd arranged, then rearranged the corporate jet for him, when it became clear earlier that day that he was not going to make the first flight as she'd scheduled it, nor the second.

He was supposed to be in Red Rock by morning where his father, William, was to be married. And even though Drew had a jet at his disposal, the earliest he'd be arriving now would be the middle of the night.

"What's the weather supposed to be like there at this time of year anyway?" She knew Red Rock was about twenty miles outside of San Antonio, but only because she'd looked for it on the map.

"Breezy with a scent of hell," he muttered.

She lifted her eyebrows a little, giving him a quick glance. "I know you're no fan of marriage—" he made that abundantly clear to every woman who passed through his revolving door "—but this is your father's wedding. Aren't you happy for him?" William Fortune had lost his wife—Drew's mother—four years earlier.

She remembered that time distinctly and not simply because she'd just begun working for Drew. It was the only time she'd ever seen him completely devastated.

It was also the only time she'd ever come close to making the mistake of forgetting that he was her boss.

Perilously close.

She blew out a silent puff of air, feeling ridiculously warm.

Four years had passed since that time, but

it might as well have been yesterday for how clear it was in her mind.

He'd kissed her.

One time.

One…very…memorable time.

And she'd been a head case for much too long afterward.

Which was all over now, thank goodness. No way would she let herself fall into the same behavior as her mother.

"No, I'm not happy." His voice was short. "And why are you nodding?"

She blinked, focusing in on the present and the look Drew was giving her. "I, um, I was just glad to be finished with the proof." She raced through the last few sentences and was relieved that it was perfect as drafted and set down her pen.

She turned to her side desk where her computer sat and moved the papers next to her. "Don't you like the woman your father is marrying?"

"Lily? She's his cousin's widow." He leaned across the desk and slid open her drawer, pulling out the cell phone. It was buzzing, yet again.

Afraid he was going to answer it, she snatched it out of his hand and slid it into the side pocket of her jacket. She definitely didn't want chancing her mother getting her boss's ear. "So?"

"So I don't see why they have to rush into anything. Wouldn't it just be easier to talk to your mother?"

She let out a faint laugh. Her fingers worked quickly over the keyboard as she made her corrections to his document. "You're obviously dreading the trip to your father's wedding. Maybe you shouldn't be giving me advice on dealing with my parent."

He exhaled roughly and shoved off the desk again. "It's not the wedding," he muttered. "Not entirely."

Her fingers slowed fractionally and realizing it, she hastened her pace again. Letting Drew get under her sympathetic nerve was not a wise course of action.

His father was getting married. Effectively replacing his mother. And Deanna had seen for herself, up close and personally, how deeply affected he'd been when she'd died.

"Your brothers will be there," she offered, trying to be helpful. He'd told her once that he had four of them, but only he and one other brother, Jeremy, didn't live in Texas. "How long's it been since you've seen them?"

"We were all in Red Rock together a few years ago."

She didn't have any siblings and so often had wished she had. She wouldn't have felt so alone in the world. "Well, then, aren't you looking forward to that?"

He swung his bat like a golf club, but he looked anything but leisurely. "What the hell does it matter?"

Irritation skittered along her nerves. "I guess it doesn't," she snapped back, "except that this whole project—" she waved her hand over the stacks of papers littering her desk "—that you insisted had to be done now, is obviously just a way for you to put off going to Texas. Were you hoping that we wouldn't actually get it finished, so you could claim that you couldn't get away at all?"

Drew nearly did a double take at his assistant's tart words. Her hazel eyes were practically snapping up at him and a blaze of color was burning in her lightly tanned cheeks.

Usually, she was the soul of calm.

And for some reason, the fact that she suddenly wasn't was just one more thorn under his saddle.

"Guess I didn't realize how important your spa weekend with the girls was," he countered.

Her lips tightened. "You know, Drew, sometimes you are such a—" She broke off and
shook her head so hard that her brownish-red
hair bounced around her shoulders. She turned
her softly pointed chin back to her computer
monitor and began typing, her fingers pounding furiously over the keys.

"A what?"

"Nothing." She was typing even faster, the
keys clicking madly.

"Just say it, Dee." He blamed the urge to
goad her even more on his father. William
wasn't satisfied with ruining his own life with
his damn marriage plans, but now he wanted
to ruin Drew's, too. "Why hold back now?"

She gave him a stern look that reminded
him, strangely enough, of his mother. Probably
because his mother was on Drew's mind, because she clearly was not on William's mind,
he reasoned.

"Why don't you just go back into your office and let me finish without distraction?" she
countered. She lifted her left hand to wave it
in dismissal, and her right hand never stopped
moving over the computer keyboard. "Decide
what you want your new business cards to
say when you replace your dad as the CEO

now that he's retiring. Maybe that will improve your mood."

"Maybe the fact that I'm not likely to be the new CEO will improve yours."

The clacking keys went abruptly silent.

She stared up at him and the fiery green glint faded in her eyes, leaving confusion in their depths. "What?"

He tightened his grip around the baseball bat.

He wanted to throw the damn thing through one of the windows.

"I'm not taking over as CEO." The words tasted like acid-coated boulders.

She looked bewildered. "But everyone knows you're taking over for him."

"Yeah, well, I guess Dad didn't read the memo." His voice was short.

"Drew—"

He exhaled. "As far as I know, he's not planning to close down this office. He just wants to close me down."

The high color faded from her cheeks and she looked pale. "But you do a remarkable job here."

"Not remarkable enough for him."

She shook her head a little, making her hair swing again. "Your father's never seemed anything but proud of the work you've done here. For heaven's sake, he even told me once when he was visiting the office how he thinks you're a chip off the old block."

"And there's the problem," he said flatly. "Since he thinks he didn't really get his act together and start up this place until he married my mother and settled down, he's gone and decided that I have to do the same damn thing!"

He swung the bat hard and it connected with the soft cushion of one of the upholstered chairs sitting outside the door to his office.

The cushion dented, and Deanna let out a startled squeak.

Neither was as satisfying as a broken window, and cursing his father, he tossed the bat onto the chair and stomped back into his office.

Deanna followed him, her hands clenched around the lapels of her drab brown jacket that matched her knee-length drab brown skirt. "Your father thinks you should get married?"

His head was pounding. He wanted a drink. He wanted a cigarette and he'd finally managed to quit the damn things six months earlier. He wanted to forget that the past year had ever happened and he particularly wanted to forget his father's ultimatum.

If only he could.

He threw himself down onto the chair behind his desk and yanked off his hat. "He doesn't just think it," he said wearily. "He expects it. Or no CEO for Drew."

She slowly sank down onto one of the chairs facing his desk. She looked dazed, which was probably the only reason she wasn't smoothing her skirt circumspectly around her pretty knees the way she usually did. "Are you sure you're not—" she swallowed and moistened her lips "—well, overreacting? Maybe you misunderstood what he meant. Maybe you heard the word *marriage* and a wire in your brain went poof."

He gave a bark of laughter that was completely devoid of humor. "Oh, he was perfectly clear. My life lacks balance, he said." He hunched forward, clenching his fists on top of his desk. "I'm too committed to the company, he said."

His fist hit the desk, sending a pen rolling off the side. "What the hell else should I be but committed? This company is everything to me and he damn well knows it. But now, dear old Dad has decided that unless my neck ends up in a marriage noose again, I'm suddenly not fit to run it after all."

Deanna's eyes were wide. "Um...again?"

He could practically feel the steam wanting to pour out of his pounding head. "And he'll go find someone who isn't even a Fortune to head things up instead." Even more than the marriage nonsense that William had been threatening for much of the past year—ever since he'd gotten involved with Lily—telling Drew just that morning that he'd bring in someone else to run the company if Drew didn't heed his words had been an even worse slam.

Their telephone conversation—if the argument that had ensued could be called that—had disintegrated from there.

Drew was still stinging from it.

"I'll be damned if I'll work for somebody else at what should be my own freaking company."

Her brows drew together, creating a little vertical line between them. "You'd just give it up, then?" She lifted her hand and tucked her hair behind her ear. "Walk away from everything you've worked for?"

"It's not like I have any women around I'd remotely consider marrying. Dad decided to marry Lily and look what happened. He's lost his marbles."

"I—I'm stunned," she said after a moment. "I don't know what to say."

He scrubbed his hands down his face and leaned back in his chair again, watching his assistant through his narrowed eyes.

But his mind was still replaying the argument with his father.

Despite his wedding to Lily scheduled for the following day—a new year and a new life with his new wife—William had had the cojones to bring up Drew's mother, Molly. To use her memory as a tool in his arsenal against Drew's footloose lifestyle.

That had been the ultimate slam.

And he'd responded in kind. If William were so concerned about Molly, then what the hell was he doing getting married again?

Drew pinched his nose and closed his eyes again. The angry words still circled in his head. "As if a marriage certificate has anything to do with success," he muttered. "It's insane." He looked at Deanna.

She was sitting straight as a poker in her chair. Instead of twisting the life out of her jacket, her hands were now twisted together in her lap. She still had that frown etched on her face and her eyes were dark with concern.

"I, um, imagine for you, marriage certainly is a deal breaker."

And Drew had never failed to close a deal.

He'd always had the singular ability to put the right pieces together, even when people—including his father—said it would be impossible.

His brain suddenly shifted. Boulders rolled and he saw a glimmer of light. "This is a deal," he murmured, wondering why he hadn't seen it before.

Maybe Deanna was right. He'd heard *marriage,* and the wiring in his brain had short-circuited.

Her eyebrows had climbed up her smooth forehead. "Excuse me?"

"A deal." He sat forward. For the first time that day he felt a grin hit him. "And all I need is a signed marriage license to seal it."

The corners of her lips curved in response to his, but she was still watching him warily. "Usually that involves a marriage," she pointed out. "Which you've already said you're not interested in."

"I'm not," he assured. "But a marriage license just comes with wedding. All I need for that is a wife."

She lifted her hands. "Exactly."

"I can hire a wife."

She blinked for a moment. "You can't possibly be serious."

"Sometimes you need specialized people at the table to close a deal. I just need the right woman to agree to the terms."

"Which are what?"

"Sign the paper, say 'I do' and then act like my wife for a short while—long enough for Dad to calm down, retire like he's planned to do all along and name me as his replacement—then go on her way."

She snorted softly and shook her head. Her hair gleamed under the overhead light. "Do I need to remind you that the women you usually date—before they reach the three-month expiration, that is—will be looking for a whole lot more out of your deal than going on her way?"

Because he usually marked his way out of his brief romantic entanglements with gifts of jewelry that Deanna arranged for him, she had a point.

"I'd need someone convincing," he mused. He drummed his fingers on the desk as his thoughts coalesced into the perfect solution.

He looked his assistant square in the eyes.

"Someone like you."

Chapter 2

Like her?

Alarm had Deanna shooting out of her chair. "Now I think you've lost your marbles."

But Drew was sitting there in his chair as calm now as he'd been agitated earlier, and she felt her stomach sink even lower when he picked up the hat he'd discarded earlier and put it on.

Backward.

The small scar near his hairline that showed because of it gave him a particularly rakish look.

"It's the perfect solution," he reasoned. The faint dimple in his cheek appeared.

She gaped. "You are mad."

He spread his hands, his palms upward. "Think it through, Dee. If a new CEO is named—someone from outside—what's the likelihood that you and everyone else who's worked here will get to stay? Bring in a new person at the top and changes are bound to trickle down. It's the nature of the beast."

A fresh wave of panic began forming at the edges of her sanity. "You already said that a new CEO wouldn't mean closing this office."

"Closing is one thing. Clearing the decks to bring in his—" he shrugged "—or her, I suppose—own people is not unusual, though. If I were going into a new place, I'd want some of my own people around me. Dad will officially be retired by then. Living permanently in Texas. He's the one ready to bring in new blood. You think he hasn't realized the ramifications to the people who've worked for him all along?"

"I can't believe that your father wouldn't have some plan for that. I've met him. He's a very caring person!"

"He's a man who has made it plain that he is starting his new life, no matter how it affects everyone else, including his own family,"

Drew said flatly, and his dimple was nowhere in evidence.

Her knees suddenly felt wobbly and she closed her hands over the back of the chair where she'd been sitting.

She needed her job. Now, more than ever.

And while she felt certain that she'd be able to find alternate work if she had to, she knew that she'd never be able to start out at the pay level that she'd risen to at Fortune Forecasting.

She wasn't getting rich by any means, but she made enough to keep her head above water…and until Gigi's latest spending jag… hers, too.

"Nobody would believe that you and I… That we…well, that we—"

"—were in love?"

She could practically see the calculating wheels turning in his mind when he picked up a pen and began drumming the end of it on his desk.

"Why not?" he asked. "I think it'll make perfect sense to anyone who bothers to think about it. My whole family knows that you're the only female who has been in my life for longer than a twelve-week stretch."

"Sure. Because you pay me well and usually leave me alone to do my job!" She shook her head. "I'm not even your type."

He looked amused and the dimple was definitely back. "And what type would that be?"

"Six feet tall, blonde and big-chested."

"Sounds like you're describing the guy who runs the magazine stand down in the lobby."

She grimaced. "Hilarious. You know exactly the kind of woman I mean. The only kind you ever date more than twice." She could count on one hand the number of women he'd seen who'd had more interest in him than the size of his bank account or what they could get out of being on Drew Fortune's arm for a while.

None of those women had ever made it past a second date with him; he'd made certain of that.

His pen was still tapping. "I do know what you mean. And you're right. You are not a gold digger," he said smoothly. "Nobody could ever make the mistake of thinking that. You've worked by my side for four years now. You're the soul of discretion, you're calm and sensible. Hell, if we're honest here, my father will probably think you're too good for me."

He made her sound like a lap dog.

She shook off the unwanted shard of pique

as she shook her head. "I can't believe I'm even standing here discussing this with you. It's insane. And I have friends still waiting for me. So am I supposed to distribute your article or was that whole episode just an exercise on your part to exert your power one last time before you take to the road?"

He ignored that. "One year of your time, Deanna, for a simple business deal. A marriage of convenience. Hands-strictly-off, right? So what's that worth to you? A raise? A promotion? A new title?"

"No! I don't want any of those things! Not when it's a simple business deal that involves getting married to you—however you want to describe it—and lying to your own father about the real reason for it!"

"And you think what he's demanding is all that reasonable?" he shot back.

She pressed her lips together. Because, if everything that Drew said was true, then of course she didn't think it was reasonable at all.

Yes, Drew played hard.

But he worked even harder.

And she'd worked for him long enough to know that there was nothing he valued more than the company that his father had founded.

She raked her hands through her hair and

turned away from the chair to pace across the office. Her knees were still shaking, but that was nothing compared to the quivering going on inside her belly.

Marry Drew Fortune?

Her?

Nerves skittered through her.

She paced back. "How do I even know that you're not exaggerating the situation?"

He gave her a look. "For what purpose? To get myself a wife? Come on, Dee."

She flushed. All right. So that was pretty unlikely, given Drew's opinion about marriage. And if he weren't practically allergic to the very idea of it, he'd have had ample opportunity to find a wife among the scores of women he'd dated. Just because she'd considered the majority of them to be shallow twits didn't mean that he had to think of them the same way.

He got up and rounded his desk and her nerves reached a screaming pitch when he dropped his arm over her shoulder.

The warmth of him seared her right through the lightweight wool of her suit and she felt like she might scream right out loud to match those nerves, note for note.

"You always play fair, Deanna," he coaxed

smoothly. "Think about all the people who're going to be affected by this."

"Don't try to schmooze me, Drew Fortune. I'm immune, remember?"

If only.

She shrugged out from beneath his easy, buddy-to-buddy arm, putting some much-needed space between them. "I've seen you in action too many times before."

"Fair enough." He exhaled and sat on the edge of his desk. "I need you, Deanna. Trust me. We can make this work."

His words sounded so sincere that he could have been trying to persuade her to marry him for real. Forever.

Her throat felt infuriatingly tight. "For a year," she reminded.

He gave a brief nod in acknowledgment. "Don't make it sound so horrible. Since the dawn of time, people have been making marriages of convenience."

She almost laughed. "Somehow I never thought that term would ever pass your lips."

He grimaced. "True enough. But my point is that plenty of people have married for reasons that had nothing to do with love."

"Well, pardon me, but I never figured that I would be one of them!"

"I never figured I'd be forced to barter for the company that I've earned the right to run with a marriage license, either. S…tuff happens."

How well she knew that.

She had only to think about her mother if she wanted proof.

He flipped off his hat and tossed it unerringly onto the iron-armed coat stand that he'd once told her had been a gift from his mother and watched her. "I don't expect you to get nothing out of this, either," he said seriously.

Which made her all the more nervous.

She had defenses against Drew the Schmoozer and Drew the Charmer. She could trade insincere banter with him until the cows came home.

But when he dropped the tactics? When he was just Drew Fortune, straight talking and perfectly sincere?

That's when she knew she was wading in waters much too deep for her peace of mind.

"I told you. There's nothing I want," she insisted.

He stood again and closed the distance between them. It took all of her willpower not to nervously back away. And when he reached out an arm toward her, she positively froze.

But all he did was reach into her pocket and withdraw her cell phone that had been buzzing almost constantly since she'd stuck it there. He held it up so that she could see the display.

Gigi, it read.

"Not even to send your mother on a vacation of her own?"

She grabbed the phone, and this time, she did power it off. Her mother could call the office line all she wanted. At the moment, Deanna considered that a lesser problem than Drew. "It would take more than a vacation to solve the matter of Gigi."

"What would it take?"

She huffed and threw out her hands. "About fifty grand." Which might as well be fifty million because it was just as unattainable. And the admission was just proof that his so-called proposal had sent her sense of discretion right into orbit and no matter what it looked like to him, she took a step backward. Then another. "So, I still need an answer about your article," she reminded, feeling almost desperate to get them back on track. Work track.

His eyes narrowed slightly. "If it's ready to send, then send it," he said after a moment.

Surprise had her feeling uneasy.

She nodded anyway, taking him at face

value and returned to her desk. Within minutes she'd sent the article off into the magical cosmos of electronic mail as well as to the newspaper editor who was printing it.

Her work done, she shut down the computer, pulled her purse out of the bottom drawer of her filing cabinet and locked up her desk.

Drew hadn't come out of his office. She could see him sitting in his chair again, but he'd swiveled it around so that he was facing the windows.

She told herself that she didn't want to be a part of his charade, but she also couldn't just walk out of the office as if nothing at all had happened. He'd been a good and fair—if sometimes challenging—boss to her. To everyone who worked in the San Diego office, for that matter.

Which was exactly the reason why they'd all been willing to give up even a portion of their holiday evening when he'd asked.

She sighed and dropped her purse next to the baseball bat on the chair he'd beat before going back into his office. She could see him reflected in the dark windows. "What are you going to do?"

He looked at the window as if it were a mirror, meeting her gaze there. "What are you going to do?" He turned in his chair until he was facing her again, and he set his own cell phone down on the center of his leather desk blotter. "Your mother lost her job again."

She looked from his phone to his face. Horror warred with anger. "What'd you do? Call her?"

"I called Joe Winston. Remember, he's the HR head over at Blake & Philips?"

Her mouth went dry. Blake & Philips was the law firm her mother had worked for… until a few months ago when she'd been fired. And the only reason that Drew knew that Gigi had worked there was because he was the one who'd told Deanna a year ago that his college buddy, Joe, was looking for legal secretaries and he knew that her mother—between jobs, again—had been worried about losing her house if she didn't find work soon.

More like Deanna was worried about her mother losing her house, because she'd been the one trying to pay Gigi's mortgage as well as her own rent.

"That was none of your business," she said stiffly.

"We're supposed to be golfing next week," he went on. "He thinks I called to tell him our tee time."

Embarrassment burned inside her. "And you just happened to mention my mother's name?"

"I didn't bring her up at all."

"Right. How else would you know?"

His gaze was steady. "You've worked for me for a while, Dee. Just because you don't go around airing your personal business as much as most of the people do around here, doesn't mean I haven't picked up some things. And your mother goes through jobs like I go through—"

"—women?" she inserted caustically.

"I was going to say shirts." He sat back in his chair, his hand slowly turning his cell phone end over end. "Joe didn't have to mention your mother. All I had to do was make an educated guess and watch your face."

Which she could feel burning now. "Fine. Yes, my mother lost her job. Again. Story of our lives." But only part of the story. "She'll find another one." She always did.

Another job. Another unattainable man to make a play for that always ended in a dramatic parting of employment when it didn't work out. Another reason to go off the financial deep end and expect Deanna to "save" her.

"Your article is sent." She pulled back her sleeve and looked at her watch. "And you're supposed to be at the airport soon. Try not to grimace all through your father's wedding tomorrow." She turned on her heel. "It'll ruin the family pictures."

"I'll give you the fifty grand." His low voice followed her.

Her feet dragged in the carpet, coming to a stop. She didn't look at him. "I shouldn't have told you that."

He was silent, but her nape prickled and she knew he'd left his desk and was walking up behind her. "You wouldn't have if you weren't upset about it."

She closed her eyes for a moment. On one hand, it was unnerving to think that he knew her that well. On the other hand, was she really surprised? There was a reason why they worked well together and she was realistic enough to know that that wasn't only because of her understanding of him. "I don't want your money."

"But do you need it?" He touched her arm, moving around until he was in front of her. "Hey." He nudged her chin until she couldn't avoid looking at him. His faint smile was crooked. And sympathetic. "I don't want to get married. But I need to."

She could feel a burning deep behind her

eyes and because she couldn't will it away, hoped to heaven that it would just stay where it was because she'd be darned if she'd cry in front of her boss. "Even if I...agreed...the money would just be a quick-fix for Gigi's problem."

"Which is what?"

She looked up at him and found her gaze trapped in his. "She has a shopping addiction."

His brows twitched together. "What?"

At least he hadn't laughed.

She sighed and moved the bat and her purse from the chair, sinking down onto it.

"A shopping addiction. And not the kind of thing people are often teasing women about, either. She doesn't just like to go out shopping for shoes or...whatever." She waved her hand. "When Gigi's...between jobs—" which in Gigi-speak really meant between the men with whom she inevitably got unwisely involved "—she gets depressed. And when she gets depressed, she shops. Online or on the home shopping networks. It doesn't matter which and it doesn't matter what. She orders stuff that she neither needs nor can afford. And it doesn't matter what I say or what I do, she won't stop and she won't get help."

She pressed her palms together, staring at

her bare fingers. "She's behind on her mortgage again, she's managed to open new credit cards that I didn't even know she had and she figures that I ought to be able to solve it all for her."

"Why you?"

"Because I've been paying things off for her since I got my first job when I was fifteen." The year her father had left. The year that Gigi started blaming Deanna for her very existence. "As long as I continue bailing her out, she's never going to get the help she needs." Deanna had finally faced that truth because she had sought the counseling that her mother refused to believe she needed.

"At least you realize that."

"Realizing it and being able to stick to it are two different things." She swallowed the knot in her throat. "It's not easy to say no to your own mother."

"It's not all that easy to say no to your father, either." He crouched down in front of her, taking her hands in his. "We can help each other here, you know."

His hands were warm and steady and nearly dwarfed hers. "It's not a, uh, a good idea. Getting involved at the workplace never is." She felt that threatening burn get even hotter.

"That's what my mother does, and it never leads to anything but disaster." Certainly not the fairy-tale wedding Gigi kept hoping for.

"People have been marrying the boss for centuries. There doesn't have to be anything wrong with that."

"Right. When the two people are actually in love." She realized her fingers had slid through his until they were twined together. She pulled her hands free and wrapped them over the arms of the chair. "And, like I said, throwing money on the situation doesn't solve the ultimate problem."

"Then we'll get your mother into counseling. For as long as it takes. Even after our arrangement is ended."

She pressed her fingers harder into the upholstery to keep them from trembling. "She'll refuse. She always does."

"We'll make sure she doesn't. We'll find a way."

"We?"

He covered her hands with his. "Yeah, we."

Her heart was climbing in her chest. She felt lightheaded. She hadn't had any support where her mother was concerned since her father walked out the door and never came back.

It had been just her.

Drew was watching her with that steady gaze and his voice, so quietly assured, was ringing in her head.

We.

The lure of that word alone seemed impossible to resist. "Okay," she whispered and felt a shudder work down her spine.

His gaze sharpened. "You'll marry me?"

She swallowed hard and had to clear her throat. "Yes."

His smile was sudden and nearly blinding. "I've always said you are the perfect assistant!" He straightened and leaned over her, pressing a fast kiss to her forehead before turning away. "This is going to work out perfectly," he was saying as he strode back into his office. "You'll come with me to Red Rock. We'll announce it there."

Deanna could hear his raised voice. Could understand his words even.

But she couldn't do much of anything but stare at her tidy desk across from her and feel the imprint of his lips as if they were still grazing her skin.

"Dee, how fast can you pack?"

She scrubbed her hands down her cheeks, attempting to drag her utterly rattled self back together. "C-couldn't you just tell your dad about us? I'd feel like I'm intruding if I go with you to Texas."

He reappeared in his doorway. The ball cap was back on his head—backward—and the dimple was back in his cheek.

He was also holding up a bottle of champagne that had been delivered that afternoon from one of his clients.

"I'm pretty sure my fiancée would be welcome at a family event," he said drily. "More than that, she'll be expected." He waved the end of the bottle in front of her. "Call the pilot again. Tell him we'll be an hour later than I planned."

Deanna felt a ridiculous surge of laughter. Or maybe it was simply that she was on the verge of hysteria.

Had she really agreed to marry him?

"I already built in an hour cushion when I rescheduled your flight the last time I talked to him," she admitted.

His eyebrows shot up. "Sounds like you were handling me." Then he grinned again. "Well done."

She managed a weak smile.

"Come on. We'll pop open this baby and celebrate. Get a few glasses, would you?" He went back into his office. "And you should let your girlfriends know you won't be making it to the spa after all."

She very nearly slapped her hand against her forehead. She'd completely forgotten about her friends. She pulled out her cell phone and turned it on again. Ignoring the little indicator that told her she had messages waiting, she quickly called Susan, the one who'd arranged the weekend, and left her own message when her friend didn't answer.

And then, holding the phone, she debated whether to call Gigi. Her mother already expected her to be gone for the long weekend. That hadn't changed, even if Deanna's destination had.

And what would she tell her mother when she did call?

That she was marrying the boss?

Gigi would probably think she'd died and gone to heaven. If she couldn't achieve that status, then at least her daughter had.

Deanna heard the distinctive sound of the champagne cork popping, and ignoring the sense of guilt she felt, she turned off her cell phone again. The only harmful thing that Gigi would do over the weekend would be to order more needless items. Items that Deanna would ensure were returned, along with all the other things she'd expected to have to deal with.

No, she'd call her mother after the holiday when she was back in town.

Maybe by then, Deanna would have figured out a way to couch her news so that Gigi wouldn't start flying over the moon.

She hurried into the small employee break room, pulled out two plastic cups from the cupboard and returned to Drew's office.

He was pulling off his linen, button-down shirt.

She nearly dropped the cups. "What are you doing?"

The shirt came off his shoulders and he balled it up, pitching it aside. The white T-shirt he was wearing beneath it clung to every centimeter of his wide chest.

"Champagne bubbled over." He picked up the bottle and she could see a ring of shimmering liquid on his desk where the bottle had been sitting. "Here." He grabbed her hand with one of the cups in it and filled it more than halfway.

"That's too much." She had to force herself not to stare at his chest. It wasn't as if she had never seen it before, and even completely, gloriously bare. When he was playing beach volleyball at their branch picnic every year, for one. But she'd never been his convenient fiancée and been faced with him less than fully dressed…

She could feel hysteria rising and ruthlessly tramped it down.

"Live a little." He was grinning as he took the second cup from her. "It's New Year's Eve."

She was glad to surrender the cup, because that meant that she could wrap both hands around her own, and maybe stop shaking like she was some schoolgirl faced with her first crush.

He filled his own cup, then held it out. "Here's to marriage."

Her stomach dipped and swayed, but she managed to give him a stern glare. "You shouldn't joke about it."

"Who's joking?" He nudged the side of his cup against hers in the toast. "At least we both know exactly what we'll be getting out of the deal. No illusions. No surprises."

"Right." She dipped her nose toward the cup. The first taste of champagne was as bitter as the nerves tightening her stomach. She swallowed it anyway.

"A ring," he said suddenly.

She looked up at him. "Excuse me?"

"We need an engagement ring." He snatched his phone off his desk again and scrolled through the phone numbers stored in it.

"You're not going to find a jeweler open on New Year's Eve," she warned. "Not even Zondervan's."

He grinned as he punched a number and held the phone to his ear. "As much business as I've given Bob Zondervan over the years? Want to bet?"

"Um…no, thanks," she managed with at least a little wisdom considering the number of orders she'd made on his behalf.

"Smart girl."

Feeling strangely weak, she sat down and shook her head.

Her mother had always told Deanna that a smart girl could catch herself the boss. Deanna had always said that would never, ever be her way.

And yet…here she was.

Her mother's daughter after all.

Chapter 3

"Come on, Sleeping Beauty. Up and at 'em." Drew nudged Deanna's shoulder.

But she just sighed and shifted, and instead of her sleeping head resting against the back-seat of the limousine that had been waiting for them when they'd landed in San Antonio, it slid sideways until it was resting on his shoulder.

Her hair smelled like green apples.

He closed his eyes for a minute, reminding himself that this was Deanna. His young assistant who was, once again, smoothing out the kinks in his life.

Yeah, okay, so she was going to get something out of it. Namely, getting some help with her crazy mother.

But as far as Drew was concerned, that was a drop in the bucket compared to what he was going to get out of it.

The right to head up Fortune Forecasting once and for all.

"Deanna." He started to reach for her hand where it was resting on her lap, but hesitated.

The diamond solitaire that he'd chosen from the two-dozen rings that Bob had brought by the office less than an hour after Drew had called him was on her ring finger. Even in the dim light in the back of the limo, the ring gleamed.

How many times had he said that a wedding ring was just a noose in disguise?

Yet now, he had a his-and-her pair of the damned things—platinum to match the band on the engagement ring—in his pocket. All ready to go for the big day.

Whenever they decided that would be.

Given the way his father was harping on the subject, it wouldn't be soon enough for William.

Drew ignored her slender fingers and jiggled her narrow wrist with the oversize watch on it instead. "Rise and shine, Dee," he said more loudly.

Her head shifted again and her eyes slowly opened. She stared at him drowsily. "Hmm?"

She'd have that expression in bed, he thought, and abruptly went hard.

An oath zipped around inside his head and he stared over her head out the window, focusing on the lines of the fencing that marked off his brother's property.

Deanna was his assistant. His fiancée for convenience's sake. Not a woman he needed to be envisioning—way too easily envisioning, at that—in his bed. Or pressed back against the deep limo seat…

"We're almost at Molly's Pride." He cleared his throat. "My brother's ranch."

She blinked a little, then seemed to realize that she was all but sprawled over the side of him, and straightened like she'd been stung by a bee.

Her hand went to her hair, smoothing it back from her face. "I fell asleep." She grimaced. "How embarrassing. I hope I wasn't drooling."

She hadn't been, but knew he was damnably on the verge of it. "Snoring, maybe," he said blandly.

She gave him a narrow look, then rolled her eyes. "I was not."

No, she hadn't been. She'd been soft and warm and the desire had hit him nearly out of the blue. He'd thought he'd conquered it a long time ago when she first started working for him. And he'd made a monumental ass out of himself by kissing her at one of the lowest points in his life.

Good assistants were hard to find.

Sexual partners weren't.

Fortunately, she'd turned her attention out the windows and he ran his hand around the back of his neck, feeling like he was ready to boil over.

"Oh, my. Is that your brother's ranch?" She was practically pressing her nose against the window like a little girl.

Only thanks to the way she'd slept for the past hour with her body snuggled up against his, he knew that beneath the shapeless green sweater she'd changed into at her apartment before they'd gone to the airport, the little girl was all woman.

"It's so beautiful." Fortunately, she was oblivious to his failure to comment. "It looks like it should be in an old movie. A Western." She looked at him over her shoulder, her smile flashing. "With John Wayne striding over to the old hacienda. I can't wait to see it when the sun is up."

Deanna was an excellent assistant and extremely good with marketing. Was it any wonder her imagination had gone into overdrive at the sight of his brother's place? "Clearly, you need more sleep."

She turned up her nose and looked out the window again. The limousine halted in front of the house with its stone entrance and Moorish-style arch and without waiting for the driver, he pushed open the door and climbed out of the car. The drive from San Antonio hadn't taken all that long, but he still felt stiff and cramped from being on the plane in the first place.

Drew liked space.

It was one of the reasons he liked living in San Diego so well. Whenever he wanted space around him, he just headed for the beach. How much more space could a man need when he was staring out at the rolling waves of the Pacific Ocean?

Still, his gaze ran over the house that his oldest brother had bought, pretty much out of the clear blue sky a few years ago, when he'd transplanted himself lock, stock and bar-

rel from Los Angeles to Texas. J.R. had given
up his position at the headquarters of Fortune
Forecasting, as well as his designer suits and
cars and coffee, in favor of jeans and cattle and
pickups. He'd also quickly turned around and
married Isabella Mendoza, who'd helped him
decorate the place.

It had been a year since Drew had last seen
Molly's Pride and even though it was well past
midnight, he could see the property and the
two-hundred-year-old hacienda gleamed with
care.

He pulled open Deanna's door and she
climbed out, her somewhat-awed gaze still focused on the house rather than Drew. Which
was a good thing because he still felt like he
was about ready to bust out of his jeans.

Maybe it would've helped if she hadn't
changed. If she'd just stayed in that boxy, ma-
tronly looking suit that she'd worn to the office.

All her suits were the same. They all dis-
guised the fact that her rear was pretty much
made for filling out a snug pair of soft blue
denims.

Annoyed with his thoughts, he left her to
gather her tote and jacket and grabbed their
few bags from the trunk when the driver

opened it. "I've got 'em. Thanks." He gave the guy a generous tip that earned him an enthusiastic smile.

"Thank you, Mr. Fortune. Happy New Year. You, too, ma'am." The driver slammed the trunk shut and quickly climbed back behind the wheel, no doubt anxious to get on with his own celebrating. A moment later, the long vehicle was driving off, leaving him and Deanna standing there alone in the moonlight.

It felt intensely…intimate. And despite the chill in the air, he felt hotter than ever.

At any other time, he would have probably found the situation ironically humorous.

Right now, he just felt like he was ready to put his head in a noose, and was almost—almost—glad to do it.

She was watching him, her eyes looking dark and mysterious, though the way she moistened her lips warned him that she was more likely just nervous as hell. "Are you sure we're doing the right thing?"

The only thing he was sure of right then was that he was having a heck of a time remembering why he should not be wanting her the way he was.

He freshened his grip on her suitcase—one of those hard-sided kind of things invented long before rollers had come along—and turned toward the arched entrance, gesturing with his chin. "Yeah. Let's go."

She moistened her lips again, leaving them even more softly shiny, and walked ahead of him through the arch that led to a massive wood door.

"Better knock," he advised. It was hours past the time he'd warned J.R. that he'd be arriving, and he figured walking in might not be such a good idea. God only knew if J.R. had taken to keeping loaded weapons at the ready along with his other Texas rancher ways...

She reached out and knocked tentatively on the door.

"Come on, Dee. They're never gonna hear that."

She gave him a look, then curled her fist and knocked harder. "Satisfied?"

Since he heard the slide of a lock a moment later, he just smiled at her. Then the door was swinging open and his brother appeared.

"About damn time," J.R. greeted, but there was still a faint smile on his face.

"Good to see you, too," Drew returned and then, because he wasn't much one for putting off the inevitable, he slid his free hand around Deanna's shoulder and felt the little start she gave. They'd have to work on that. "You remember my assistant, Deanna," he began. J.R. nodded. "We're late because just tonight, she agreed to marry me."

A full heartbeat of silence followed his abrupt announcement.

Then J.R.'s smile became a little more broad, though Drew recognized the disbelief in his brother's hazel eyes, as he turned his focus on Deanna. "Well, then," J.R. said smoothly, "that sure does make up for the pip-squeak's tardiness." He reached out and took the tote bag that was slung over Deanna's shoulder and wrapped his hand around her elbow, drawing her inside.

"Pip-squeak?" Deanna laughed a little and looked over her shoulder at Drew.

"Better than runt," he muttered. "That's what he used to call Darr." Two years younger than Drew, Darr was the baby of the family. He was also a firefighter and could probably take them all down without breaking a sweat.

"You're all still on the easy side of forty," J.R. was saying, as he chuckled and wrapped an arm around Drew's neck, hugging him hard. "So I'll call you whatever the heck I want. Damn, it's good to see you." Just as abruptly, he was pushing Drew away and taking Deanna's cumbersome suitcase. "Even if I was beginning to wonder if you were going to get here before dawn or not."

He turned and headed barefoot along the distressed wood floor through the silent house. "Isabella stayed up for a while but finally bit the dust a few hours ago." He looked over his shoulder at Deanna. "My wife."

Deanna nodded. "Drew's told me about her. I hope I'm not putting you out too badly. I warned Drew that he should have called ahead to let you know I was coming with him."

"Don't you worry any about that," J.R. assured. "We're glad to have you." He grinned. "Particularly when you're brave enough to take on our Andrew, there. And what's better to have around for a wedding than more family?"

Drew could see the color come into her cheeks.

"You're very gracious."

"My wife would kick me otherwise," J.R. assured. He turned down a hall. "Jeremy's out for the count, too." He jerked his chin. "He's in that room there at the end of the hall. Got in yesterday."

Deanna's wide gaze was taking in the white plaster walls around them, which Drew knew were relatively fresh even if they did look authentic to the old house. "Is that one of your wife's tapestries?" She pointed to a colorful weaving on one wall as they passed it. "Drew's told me what a talented artist she is."

J.R. nodded and the look of pride on his face was plain to see. "There's not a corner of this place where she hasn't made her mark," he said before pushing open a door. "You'll be in here." He stepped aside and hopefully missed the panicked glance that Deanna threw in Drew's direction as she entered the bedroom.

The most notable feature was the wide bed that took up a good portion of the space.

His damnable body stirred again and he felt heat start to climb up his neck when his gaze ran into J.R.'s. "Looks comfortable," he said, ignoring the heat both in his neck and in his gut, and went into the room behind her.

He dropped his duffel and suit bag on the white comforter covering the bed and watched Deanna's fingertips gently graze the petals of one of the roses clustered in a vase on the chest of drawers next to one of the windows. Her reflection jumped back at him from the big, heavily framed mirror that sat on the floor against the wall across from the bed. Next to that was a fireplace where logs were already placed, just waiting for a match.

Her auburn hair was tousled around her shoulders and her expression was almost unbearably soft as she touched the flowers.

He felt a bead of sweat angling down his spine. He shrugged out of the leather bomber jacket and pitched it across a chair in the corner that sat next to a small table with a reading lamp.

His brother had a faint smile on his lips as he ambled into the room after them. He set Deanna's suitcase on the floor at the foot of the bed. "Bathroom's attached through there," he gestured. "Extra blankets and pillows are in the closet, there. If you need anything else, just yell."

Drew figured that what Deanna needed was a separate bedroom, and was grateful as all get-out when she only smiled and quietly told his brother that everything was lovely and she was certain they'd be just fine.

"Right, then. See you at breakfast." J.R. stepped out of the room. He grinned. "Or not." He reached for the door and pulled it closed.

Alone, Deanna turned away from the pink roses and looked at Drew.

"I can't help it," he said in a low voice.

"What do you want me to do? Tell him we don't sleep together?"

She made a face. "He'd never believe you weren't sleeping with any woman you brought with you, much less your own fiancée."

He almost felt himself flush, which was stupid. He was no kid. Of course he had sex with the women he saw.

That was pretty much all he had with the women he saw. It wasn't as if he was looking for a partner in life after all.

"Then I'll sleep on the floor if it makes you feel better."

"Not exactly comfy." She tapped her soft-soled boot on the hardwood floor and let out a huge breath. "We'll just have to make do with the bed." She shook her head and looked away. "At least it's huge," she added. "You could sleep a family of five in that thing."

It was definitely an exaggeration, but he let it pass. Because whatever she wanted to think, there would still only be the two of them on that soft-looking mattress.

And his imagination was becoming increasingly fertile.

Her hair would look like burning embers against that white, white comforter...

He cleared his throat a lot more easily than

he did the images from his head. "It's been a long night. You go ahead and—" he waved toward the bed "—you know, go to sleep. I'm still too keyed up anyway. I'm going to go find J.R.'s whiskey."

The relief that filled her eyes would have been comical if it weren't so deflating. Just because—at the moment—he was having a hard time remembering the purpose of their engagement didn't mean that she was having the same problem.

"If you're sure..." She left the words hanging and he made himself nod.

He needed to be remembering how she'd acted the last time he'd been uncontrolled enough to kiss her and not how she'd felt, pressed against him in the limo.

Then she'd been clearly appalled, and he knew to this day that the only reason she hadn't quit on the spot was that she'd felt sorry for him because his mother had just died. That, and the fact that he'd sworn to her it would never happen again.

"Yeah," he lied. "I'm sure. Get some sleep. Tomorrow will be a busy day."

She looked at her watch. "Today will be a busy day, actually."

"Right. Today." He reached for the doorknob and quietly turned it. "Happy New Year, Dee."

Deanna's smile felt almost as shaky as her knees.

She knew it was best if he left for a little while, but a strong part of her wanted to ask him not to.

And that fact alone was reason enough to need some distance from her boss-slash-fiancé, even if it were only for a few minutes. So she kept the words to herself. "Happy New Year, Drew."

And then he was stepping out of the room, closing the door silently behind him.

Once he was gone, Deanna's smile died and she drew in a deep breath.

Without his intoxicating presence, the room felt as spacious as her common sense told her it actually was. It was only when she was closed in with him that it seemed as if the walls were only two inches from that big... wide...bed.

She caught her reflection in the oversize mirror. "This is what you get for making rash decisions," she whispered to herself.

The only response she got was her own glazed-looking expression staring back at her.

The silence of the house seemed to tick like

the hands of a clock, and she grabbed her suitcase, hefting it onto the foot of the bed. Drew had given her a reprieve of sorts and she knew she'd better darn well use it wisely. The last thing she wanted was for him to come back and find her still standing around like some ninny who was afraid to climb into bed for what was left of a night's sleep.

She unfastened the stiff latches and flipped open the case, taking out the dress that she'd added on top of her other clothing. When they'd stopped at her apartment on the way to the airport, she'd done her level best to discourage Drew from accompanying her inside. But the man simply hadn't taken the hint and she hadn't exactly known how to tell him flat-out to stay in the car when she couldn't even come up with a plausible excuse.

So he'd walked up the iron-and-cement flight of stairs to her door and had braced herself for his comments when she'd let them in.

But all he'd done was silently glance over the stacks of shipping boxes that were crammed into her dining room, covering the floor and the small table and even the end of the couch. Boxes containing every item imaginable from small travel-size baby-food mills to closet organizers and exercise equipment that she'd taken from her mother's home to send back to the companies from which Gigi had ordered them.

He hadn't gaped. He hadn't even raised his eyebrows.

She'd been so grateful for that that she hadn't even thought to protest when he'd followed her down the short hallway to stand in the doorway of her bedroom while she'd opened her ancient suitcase that had already been packed for her spa weekend.

He'd told her that they would be in Texas for four days—through the weekend, and returning to San Diego on Wednesday. That didn't necessitate a lot of clothing, fortunately, because she didn't have much in her wardrobe that wasn't either kick-around-the house casual, or wear-to-work professional. She had sweats that she wore to the gym where she coached girls' volleyball in exchange for her membership fee, and she had jeans and shorts and suits.

But there wasn't much call for her to own dresses suitable for an afternoon wedding, and when she'd scooted through her assortment of hangers for the second time without finding anything she could imagine wearing, she'd looked over her shoulder at him and told him that he would be better off going to Texas alone. He could announce their engagement without her being there, couldn't he?

But he'd just given her that Drew look, the one that saw right through her excuses, and told her to pack one of her suits and to stop worrying about it.

"I'm not wearing something like this to a wedding." She'd shrugged out of her blazer and shook it at him. "This is for work."

"Well, even that might be debatable," he'd drawled, and had joined her in front of her tight closet. He'd reached in and pulled out a frothy thing shoved far to the side. "Wear this, then."

"What's that supposed to mean?"

"It means," he'd held the hanger up against her shoulders. "It doesn't look like something you'd wear to work. So? Good for a wedding or not?"

She hadn't been thinking about the dress. She'd been thinking about his comment about her suits. They fit and they were professional-looking and the complete opposite of the short skirts and clingy blouses that her fashionista mother preferred.

But knowing that the jet was waiting for them and not wanting to be the cause of their being any later than they already were, she hadn't pursued the matter.

And now, she held the dress up to her shoulders in much the same way that Drew had, and turned to look at herself in the mirror.

It was a vivid, bright pink for one thing, and with her hair, that wasn't a color she ever wore.

For another, it was ruffled.

Well, not exactly ruffled. The skirt was just made of dozens of pieces of fabric that all seemed to float independently of each other, making it look like it rippled even when she was holding it still. And the narrow, halter-style bodice was snug. And low.

She'd never worn it before.

For that matter, she hadn't bought it.

Gigi had. She'd given it to Deanna for her last birthday, and when Deanna had protested that it was too expensive—a more tolerable excuse than that the dress simply wasn't to Deanna's taste—her mother had produced the receipt to prove that the clearance-priced dress wasn't returnable. She'd lamented how her little Deedee just thrived on thwarting her and in the end, rather than go to battle over what was supposed to be a birthday gift, Deanna had taken the dress and put it in the back of her closet.

Where it had stayed. Lurking, as if it had been biding its time, waiting for Drew Fortune to find there.

Even as tired as she was, Deanna recognized the ridiculousness of the notion and she rubbed her eyes. At least the dress had come with a matching wrap. It was thin and almost translucent, but it would cover up her bare shoulders.

And as much as she didn't want to wear a dress chosen by her mother, she did have to admit that it was more suitable for the occasion than anything else her closet had contained. So she hung up the dress and its wrap behind the door that J.R. had indicated, and she made quick work of unpacking the rest of her items, most of which she left folded and tucked in one of the empty chest drawers. When the suitcase was empty, she wedged it out of the way in one corner of the closet on the floor, hung Drew's garment bag on the rack as far from her dress as was physically possible, and then turned to ponder his well-used duffel bag that was still sitting on the bed.

As his assistant, she really shouldn't have had any issue with simply unpacking his things for him. And as his fiancée, if she were one of the true variety, she wouldn't have had any issue, either.

Instead, she stared at the thing as if it would singe her fingers raw if she dared to unzip it.

In the end, she chickened out of dealing with it entirely, and transferred it from the foot of the bed to the chair in the corner.

Then she carried her small tote bag into the attached bathroom where she quickly washed her face and cleaned her teeth, changed into her cotton tank top and flannel pajama pants, and padded barefoot back to the bed.

Which side of the bed did Drew like?

She felt her skin flush just from having the question enter her mind and chewing on her lip, she jerked back the downy-light comforter to reveal crisp white sheets with a lovely embroidered edge.

She would have sighed with purely feminine appreciation for the beautiful, luxurious bedding if her heart hadn't felt like it had climbed up into her throat. As it was, she climbed into bed, keeping so close to the edge of the mattress that she was in danger of rolling off, only to realize that she'd forgotten to turn off the light.

She got out of bed again, turned on the light in the bathroom and pulled the door nearly closed so there was only a sliver of light showing, then turned off the bedroom lamp and returned to bed.

Her head sank into the fluffy pillows and she determinedly closed her eyes.

The image of Drew's face seemed burned into the back of her eyelids and she opened them again.

She was tired right down to her bones for a whole host of reasons, not the least of which was her boss.

Who was, sooner or later, going to be sharing this very bed with her.

She dragged the comforter up to her chin, but it still didn't block out the reality of it all and she trembled so hard suddenly that it was a wonder the bed didn't vibrate from it.

At this rate, it was going to be a very long four days.

Chapter 4

"Guess you found what you were looking for." J.R.'s voice was quiet behind Drew where he was sitting in an alcove that overlooked the outdoor courtyard at the center of the house.

"You always do have the good stuff." Drew picked up the decanter of amber liquid and poured another finger into his squat, crystal glass. "Texas hasn't changed that, at least."

"Don't know what you have against Texas." J.R. folded his long body into a leather side chair. "You used to enjoy coming to Red Rock when you were a kid, too."

There'd been a lot of summer visits to the

Double Crown Ranch where their father's cousin Ryan, and his wife, Lily, lived.

"Riding horses and fishing and playing at cowboy was all right when I was ten." Warmth slid down his throat as he sipped his brother's fine whiskey. "I still can't believe you gave up everything in L.A. to come and live here." If his brother hadn't resigned from Fortune Forecasting, he would have been in line to run the place.

Drew couldn't help wondering if William would have demanded that his eldest son toe up to the marriage line before handing the company over, or not.

But J.R. had resigned. He'd walked away from it all, so the question was now moot.

"I gained everything that matters to me when I came to Red Rock," J.R. said quietly.

"You mean Isabella, I suppose. But you barely knew her before you moved here."

His brother shrugged. "Isabella. The ranch. California was fine for its time, but this is home now. I can't imagine life anywhere else."

"You sound like you're channeling Dad," Drew muttered. He swirled the glass, watching the liquid glisten in the light from the small lamp he'd turned on next to his chair. "He acts as if life didn't begin for him until he left California, too."

He heard J.R. sigh. "That's not it at all."

"Isn't it?" Drew looked over at his brother. J.R. was forty-two, married to a woman ten years younger. Their father was seventy-five, still fit and still hardy—and planning to marry a woman ten years younger. "He had a life in California. Now he acts as if none of it matters."

"He acts as if he's ready to move on and live the rest of his life," J.R. countered. "Face it, Drew. He's happy. And just because he's marrying Lily doesn't mean he's forgotten Mom."

Drew stiffened. He didn't want to discuss their mother. He particularly didn't want to think about the way William had thrown her memory in his face that morning when they'd argued about the company.

Strike that.

Yesterday morning.

It was past midnight. Officially New Year's Day.

And their father's wedding day.

He scrubbed his hand down his face and tossed back the rest of his drink.

"So for a guy who's been allergic to marriage ever since you told us things didn't work out the first time, how'd you come to be engaged to your assistant?"

Drew should have known better than to expect his brother to accept his engagement at face value and he supposed it was just as well to get some practice in early, before he faced the rest of the family—and their father—later that day at the wedding. "When you meet the right one, it doesn't matter what you thought you believed." It was true enough in a sense.

It was also something that his mother had told him more than once since his first—and until now, only—attempt at wedded bliss had quickly and miserably failed.

He could feel the weight of J.R.'s gaze.

"How soon did you know that Isabella was the right woman for you?"

"Almost immediately," J.R. said easily.

"So I'm not as quick on the uptake as you are."

"Hmm."

His brother's speculative tone made Drew warier than ever and he hunched forward and pushed out of the deep chair. "Guess I'd better let you catch some z's before breakfast." He lifted his empty glass. "Thanks for the hot milk."

He caught the wry tilt of J.R.'s smile from

the corner of his eye as he headed back to the bedroom, stopping off at the kitchen only long enough to set his glass in the sink.

Unfortunately, the anesthetizing effects of his brother's expensive booze evaporated when Drew made it to the bedroom and silently pushed open the door.

The faint light from the bathroom cast a glow over the bed, but the bump of Deanna beneath the fluffy comforter on the side closest to the bathroom was barely visible, except for the cascade of her dark hair across the pillow. The sight did a bang-up job of refreshing the images that had sent him running out of the damn room in the first place.

He stood in the doorway for a while, waiting for her head to lift or for her to make some noise to indicate whether she was awake and knew he was hovering there.

But there wasn't the faintest whisper of movement from the bed and he figured that he'd better get inside the room before the breakfast bacon started sizzling. So he quietly stepped into the room and shut the door.

He'd never gone to such trouble before to keep a woman from waking. He'd never brought a woman to his own place in San

Diego. It was always easier to go to hers, simply because it was always easier to leave.

He could make out the shape of his duffel bag sitting on the chair in the corner and it was only then that he realized he hadn't bothered packing any sort of pajamas or robe. He generally didn't bother with either, and when he'd shoved his clothes into his bag in the morning before going to the office, he certainly hadn't expected to be bringing a fiancée along.

He shoved his hands through his hair and wanted to curse all over again at the situation his father had created. He unbuttoned his shirt and tossed it on the chair and winced at the thud of his shoes on the floor and jangling of his belt buckle when his pants followed the shirt.

He looked over at the bed.

Still no movement, thank God.

He wasn't sure how his ordinarily unflappable assistant would react if she woke up and saw him standing like a fool next to the bed, wearing nothing but his boxers and an erection, particularly after he'd assured her more times than he could count that their union would be entirely hands-off.

He let out a long breath and carefully lifted

back the comforter and sheet and sat on the side of the bed. She still didn't move.

He rolled his eyes heavenward. If anyone who knew him could see him now, he'd never live it down.

Still moving at the speed of a sloth, he managed to stretch out on the mattress. More importantly, he managed not to groan in appreciation of the comfortable bed after the long, trying day.

He drew the covers over him and stared up into the dark shadows of the beamed ceiling.

He'd thought that once he got to Red Rock, the only thing he'd be able to think about was the looming specter of his dad getting married. But the warm presence of the woman lying within arm's reach of him had taken front and center. And as comfortable as the bed was, he figured it'd be highly unlikely for him to get any sleep that day.

He sighed and stretched out a little more, throwing his arm over his head and his knuckles accidentally rapped against the antique headboard.

The bedding rustled next to him and he clenched his teeth so tightly he'd probably need dental work.

"Drew?"

A fresh litany of curses went through his brain. "Sorry. Didn't mean to wake you up."

She turned on her side to face him and bunched her pillow under her cheek. He could feel her gaze as acutely as if she were pressing her cheek against him. "Are you all right?"

He was going to hell, sure as the sun was going to rise in a few hours, that's how he was. "I'm fine." His voice was short. "Go back to sleep."

Of course, she didn't. And the shadowed weight of her gaze simply continued boring into him.

He could stop that, simply enough. Just roll over and pull her into his arms. That would send her scurrying back to her own corner of the bed for certain.

"People get up early around here," he finally warned.

"I get up early at home." Her voice was even. "And much as I'd like to sleep, somehow it's difficult when you're two feet away, simmering like a pot on the stove."

There wasn't two feet between them. Not even close.

Drew would be better off if there were.

He even found himself strongly considering the wisdom of sleeping on the floor, but was damned if he'd move now. Who knew what she'd end up making of that.

"I'm not simmering," he muttered. A patent lie that she had the nerve to actually snort softly over.

Then she was shifting again, turning onto her back. She smoothed the comforter under her arms and he realized they were bare. He could see the creamy sheen of her skin from her fingertips right up her arms and over the curve of her shoulders until her hair blocked the view.

He closed his eyes.

Yup. Open the doors to Hades. He was moving in.

"Your brother has a really nice home."

"Yeah."

Merciful silence ticked for a few seconds.

"How much older is he than you?"

"Eight years."

"And your other brothers?"

He sighed. "You're not going to go to sleep, are you."

"Are you?"

He doubted the reasons for their wakefulness were even in the same library much less on the same page. "Nick's thirty-nine. He and Charlene have a baby. Matthew." The pictures that Nick emailed him of the little guy were cute as hell, even though Drew still had a hard time envisioning his brother as a family man. Drew had his reasons for being wary of marriage, but Nick had been a diehard bachelor from the womb. "He's a financial analyst at the Fortune Foundation."

Deanna shifted again. Now she was looking at him once more, her head propped on her hand.

The comforter fell away enough for him to realize she was wearing some skinny-strapped thing that was almost as pale as her skin.

And it didn't hide a damn thing the way her boxy suits did. The swell of her breasts was apparent.

He figured he ought to be grateful that the light from the bathroom was as faint as it was. But a strong part of him was wishing it weren't.

Which just proved what a hell-bound dog he was.

"That's a philanthropic organization, right?"

Who knew she'd be such a chatty Cathy in the wee hours of the morning when she was generally pretty quiet in the office?

Feeling way too warm, he shoved back the comforter, but kept the sheet in place. The light was dim, but he wasn't going to take any chances.

And every time he thought the simmering want inside of him was going to settle and cool down, something—like that clinging shirt of hers—just fueled the fire all over again.

"The foundation was begun in memory of Ryan Fortune. My dad's cousin." And his dad's fiancée's deceased husband.

He felt his jaw tighten again. Maybe his father should be worrying about how that would have sat with his wife instead of tossing her memory into Drew's face.

"Did you know him well?"

He dragged his thoughts together. "Well enough, I guess. Ryan was a good guy. Believed in good things. He was always trying to help others. Sharing what he considered his own good fortune. Maybe he's up there somewhere watching what the foundation does now." He didn't want to think what Ryan might be thinking about his own cousin marrying his wife. "The agency has grown a helluva lot more than anyone ever expected. It started out as a small storefront and now they've got a big building on the highway just outside of Red Rock."

"What about your other brothers?"

Fortunately, they were easier subjects. "Jeremy's three years older than me. You'll meet him at breakfast, no doubt. I'll be surprised if he stays past tonight after the wedding, though. Hardly anything keeps him away from his practice in Sacramento. He's an orthopedic surgeon." And no happier about William's impending marriage than Drew was.

"He's not married either, right?"

"Nope." Not for lack of trying from plenty of women, though, who seemed to find his workaholic brother's blue eyes as irresistible as his status as a surgeon.

"Then there's you," she quickly dipped her chin, nodding toward him.

The faint scent of green apple taunted him. "And Darr brings up the rear," he added abruptly.

"The firefighter."

"Yeah. He and Bethany have a little girl named Randi." Another cutie who looked just like her mother with wavy blond hair and big blue eyes.

He could appreciate cute kids as long as they weren't his own. Being an uncle suited him just fine.

"And who else should I know when we go to the wedding?"

"Does it matter?"

"It does if you want anyone to believe we're really…involved." She said the word as if it were something that should only be voiced if you were wearing hazmat gear.

He could relate.

"What about Lily?" she continued. "The bride? She was married to Ryan Fortune and you've said that he was a good guy. What's she like?"

Drew had liked her just fine until his dad had lost all sense over her. "I always thought she was devastated when Ryan died."

"How long ago was that?"

He didn't even have to calculate. "Six years ago." Just two years before his mother had died.

And not long after that, neither Lily's nor William's supposed devastation over the losses of their spouses had seemed to matter quite so much.

They'd gotten involved and according to his father, William would have married Lily a year ago if it weren't for Lily's insistence that they give Drew and his brothers some time to adjust to the situation.

As if that was likely to happen.

"Will it be a large wedding?"

"There's likely to be a lot of guests, I suppose."

"You don't know?"

"It's not like I'm supposed to stand up there with them. J.R.'s acting as his best man."

"That's nice." She lowered her head finally, resting it on her arm on top of the pillow. "You, um, seem to get along well with J.R."

"Yeah."

"And your other brothers?"

"Yeah." He wondered where she was heading.

But all she did was make a soft little sound that had a ripple working down his spine. "I always thought it would be nice to have a large family."

"Growing up, it had its moments," he allowed. And even though they'd all kind of gone along their own paths when they'd become adults, Drew supposed he was still pretty close to his brothers. They might not see each other all that often—not with J.R. and Nick and Darr all living in Red Rock, while he and Jeremy were still in California—but they managed to keep up with each other's lives all the same.

"There are a boatload of cousins, too," he added. "My dad's brother Patrick and his wife and all of them will probably be around. You won't get a chance to meet my aunt Cindy, though." He hadn't asked for details about the wedding, but William had offered up that information. "She's only a few years younger than dad, but she's probably still out there sowing wild oats somewhere. Total character." It was easy enough to appreciate when she was his aunt. As a mother to her four kids, though, Drew knew she'd seriously left something to be desired. Nurturing, she wasn't.

Which made him think about Deanna's mother. "What are you going to tell your mother?"

She rolled onto her back again and pulled the comforter up to her chin. "Nothing until I have to." She evidently didn't feel like she was in danger of overheating just because they were in the same bed. "And then nothing more than I have to."

He very nearly asked her then about her father, but she yawned widely and rolled again, until her back was toward him and he swallowed his curiosity. As far as he could recall, he'd never heard Deanna mention the man.

He didn't know if her father was alive or dead or even if he'd ever been a part of her life at all.

When it came down to it, his assistant knew a lot more about his life than he did about hers.

It wasn't a point that had ever bothered him much before, but now, it niggled at him.

But he said no more about it. He and Deanna might not be involved "that" way, but he was smart enough to know that when a woman—any woman—turned her back like that, it was definitely the end of the conversation as far as she was concerned.

So he just stared into the shadows until he heard the cadence of her breathing finally change. Slow. Lengthen.

Only then did he finally manage to close his eyes and get some peace from his troubled thoughts. But a short while later, when he felt the soft shape of his sleeping companion brush against him, he was wide-awake again.

And his troublesome body seemed doomed to keep him there.

She was roasting.

Deanna kicked at her blankets, only realizing when her bare feet encountered the silky smooth texture of expensive cotton sheets that she wasn't in her own bed in her own apartment.

She went stock still, staring at the window across from her.

Shutters were closed across it, but sunlight was sneaking around the dark, wood slats.

It wasn't the sunlight that had her attention, though.

It was the warm, hair-roughened, sinewy arm that was lying heavily over her waist. And it was the long-fingered hand that belonged to that arm that was cupping her breast.

She sank her teeth into her bottom lip. She would have held her breath, if she could. But her heart was suddenly pounding so fast that she didn't seem able to even accomplish that.

But when she realized that her nipples were tightening and Drew's thumb was lazily brushing across it, she gingerly wrapped her hand around his wrist and started to push his hand away from her.

He mumbled something and simply tightened his arm around her waist and she found herself sliding against the smooth sheet until the entire back side of her was pressed against him.

She might have taken comfort in the fact that his hand had strayed away from her breast to press flat against her belly, except that it had snuck beneath the edge of her camisole and was pressing flat against her bare skin.

And all of him was pressing hard against the back of her.

She swallowed a squeak and scrabbled at his arm again. "Let go."

He mumbled something again, then his arm mercifully lightened up around her as he rolled back. "Geez, Dee. Can't you let a guy sleep?"

She scrambled out of the bed, dragging down the hem of her camisole with one hand and shoving back her tumbled hair with her other. The diamond ring on her finger felt heavy and wholly unfamiliar as it tangled in her hair.

"Don't geez me," she countered, yanking her hand free. "What is wrong with you?"

His hair was falling over his forehead and his angular jaw was heavily shadowed. Against the backdrop of the pristine, white bedding, he looked dark and dangerous and utterly, totally seductive. Particularly when he focused a heavy-lidded gaze on her face. The corner of his lips kicked up, adding to his devilish appeal. "Evidently, nothing."

Her cheeks felt as if they were on fire. She wasn't naive enough to think that she, personally, had anything to do with that…well…what she'd felt pressing insistently against her back-side. "Obviously, we'll have to do something about, um, about this."

He lifted an eyebrow. "Oh, yeah?"

She flushed even harder. "Not that."

"This. That." His grin widened. "You've always been so good with descriptions, Dee, but right now you're outdoing yourself."

She crossed her arms tightly, even though it was too late to hope that he hadn't already taken in the rigid points of her nipples that she knew had to be plainly visible through the snug cotton knit of her cami. For heaven's sake, he'd had his hand there! "I'm glad that you're so amused by me. You know good and well I meant our sleeping arrangements."

He smiled outright, and annoyed as much with him as she was with her damnable weakness where he was concerned, she huffed and strode into the bathroom, slamming the door shut behind her.

When she heard his laugh through the door, she would have locked it, too, if the thing had possessed one.

Instead, she caught her reflection in the mirror over the sink.

"You are in trouble here," she accused softly.

"Did you say something?"

She nearly jumped out of her skin. Drew's voice was so clear she suspected he was standing right on the other side of the door. "No!"

"Sounded like you did."

She felt around the entire door handle and still found no lock. He wouldn't walk in on her, would he?

It seemed unfathomable.

But then she never could have imagined that she'd wake up with his arms wrapped around her body, either.

Well, no. That wasn't strictly true, either. She could imagine it.

But she just hadn't really expected it to ever happen.

"Deanna?"

She swallowed and raked her hair back from her face. "I, um—" She cleared her throat and spoke a little more loudly. "I was just promising myself coffee soon." She winced at the poor excuse. She didn't even drink coffee.

"O-kay." He plainly didn't believe her, but at least he didn't make more of the matter than he already had. "I'm gonna go see if we slept right through breakfast."

"All right." She turned on the tap and water rushed into the sink, but she crept back to the door and listened against it. She felt like an idiot, but she didn't relax the least bit until she heard the sound of the bedroom door creaking open and then closing again.

She very nearly slid down the wall into a pile of mush.

Only the fear that he could be back sooner rather than later kept her moving and she practically tore open her tote bag, pulling out her shampoo and cosmetics. She raced through the shower, barely allowing herself enough time to appreciate the luxurious spray of water—twice as hot and twice as full as her miserly shower back home—before she was stepping out again onto the thick, woven bath mat. She wrapped a fluffy white towel around herself and tucked in the end as tightly as the plush thickness would allow.

She raked the tangles out of her hair with her comb and managed to put on her makeup using the only corner of the mirror that hadn't steamed up. Not that she wore much in the way of makeup. She rarely did. But there was to be a wedding that day, so she added a touch more eye shadow and blush than she normally used, and hoped it was good enough to cover the fact that there were shadowy circles under her eyes from too little sleep.

Fortunately, there was still no sound of

Drew's return and she plugged in her blow-dryer and made just as fast work out of getting her thick hair dry and lying smooth and flat against her shoulders. It was actually a little long. She was long overdue for a trim, but she'd been saving up for her New Year's weekend with her friends.

So much for that.

She tucked everything back into her small tote and stowed it on the empty shelf below the one that held the towels and walked back into the bedroom, tightening the towel again. She was just pulling fresh panties out of the drawer where she'd stowed them when the bedroom door creaked softly and she whirled around.

Drew, wearing jeans and nothing else, gave her a look that seemed just as shocked.

"Coffee," he muttered and extended his arm and the sturdy, brilliant red mug he was holding.

She'd worked for the man for four years. She'd personally fixed and served him countless pots of coffee during that time. Knew that he liked it stronger than most people preferred, and that only when he was nursing a hangover did he want any sugar added.

Clearly, he'd never noticed that not once had she ever had any coffee herself.

But that's what she got for lying.

If the worst thing that happened that week-end was having to choke down a cup of the vile stuff, she supposed it was a small price to pay, particularly when a part of her was ogling the hard, cut lines of his abdomen.

So she managed a smile and reached out to take the mug, only realizing then that her panties were still clutched in her fist. She flushed and pitched them back into the drawer then reached for the coffee mug again. "Thanks."

Unfortunately, when she reached, the tucked towel gave way.

And all she could do was stand there, frozen, as the thick, thick towel fell right to the hardwood floor beneath her bare feet.

Chapter 5

Hell and damnation.

The oath exploded inside Drew's head just as quickly as it passed his lips when that white towel seemed to hit the ground almost in slow motion where it mounded around Deanna's bare feet and slender ankles.

He knew only a second had passed before they were both reaching down for the thing, but what he'd seen in that second was blistered into his brain.

No. Not even blistered. Because a blister would heal and disappear.

More like tattooed.

Because the image of her sleek figure was not likely to leave his mind. Ever.

His hand reached the towel, only to collide with hers. Realizing his gaze was straying back to the expanse of creamy, tanned skin that covered her from shoulders to toes—save a few intriguingly tiny, pale triangles—he let her take the towel as they straightened, and instead concentrated on the depths of the rich coffee that Isabella had prepared. He never would have figured his assistant for a bikini type, but he damn sure could recognize the source of those tan lines.

"Sorry." His voice came out like chunks of gravel, and he coughed. "I didn't mean to startle you."

Deanna was looking anywhere but at him. She was holding the towel so tightly around herself that her fingers were nearly white. "No. It's my fault. I, um, I—" she broke off and shook her head. Her hair bounced against her bare shoulders. "This is what I get for lying," she mumbled.

"It was a simple accident." He reached past her, aware of the way she jumped when he did so, and set the coffee mug on top of the chest. "Once we're married and living together—"

"Living together!"

He frowned, looking through the half-closed door out into the hallway. Fortunately, the only sounds he could hear were the laughter and voices coming from the other side of the house where everyone else was still gathered in the kitchen.

He closed the door.

"Yeah, living together." Only by some pity from God was he able to keep his eyes focused on her face. "That's what generally happens when couples marry." He kept his voice low. The adobe-looking walls were probably thick here, but he didn't want to take any chances.

"We—" her free hand waved between them "—are not a couple," she reminded.

He caught that waving hand and held it up between them. The diamond on her finger sent prisms of light dancing around the walls. "For all intents and purposes, we became one when I put this rock on your finger. What the hell kind of marriage do you think it would look like we have if we don't live together after the I dos? For that matter, it's already striking some of them as odd that we're not already doing so."

She yanked her hand out of his. "Tell them I'm old-fashioned." Her voice was shaky and she looked away from him again only to suddenly shove the chest drawer closed.

But that was a little like trying to undo the whole towel-drop thing.

He'd already seen the hanks of ribbon and sheer lace lying neatly inside.

And because he'd seen, up close and personally, the stunningly perfect body they'd be covering, he had a double dose of fresh torment for his overactive mind.

"That's exactly what I told Jeremy," he said. "That you're old-fashioned." And for some reason, his brother had found that statement riotously funny.

Isabella had simply smiled serenely as she'd set a platter of bacon and sausage on the table between them that she and Evie—the housekeeper and cook that his brother had brought with him from L.A.—had reheated for him because he'd overslept everyone else by a good three hours, and said she thought "old-fashioned" was still a good trait to possess.

"Great." Deanna made a face. "Now they'll wonder even more what on earth you're doing, supposedly marrying me."

"What do you want me to say, Deanna?" He was frustrated on so many levels that he couldn't keep it out of his voice.

"I don't know!" She turned away, still clutching the towel around her like a drowning person clutched a life vest. She sat down on the edge of the bed, only to bounce back up and move away from it, too.

Irritation joined frustration. "I'm not likely to attack you, for God's sake. Just because we woke up the way we did doesn't mean I don't have some self-control."

"I didn't say you didn't."

"You were the one cozying up to me in your sleep, you know," he added. "Now you're acting like a virginal nun who's afraid to be alone with a man."

She went red. The color spread from the tips of her ears behind which she'd tucked her shining hair to the hollow at the base of her throat, over her smooth, toned shoulders and right down beyond the edge of the towel cinched above her breasts.

He actually found himself watching her shapely calves below the towel to see if she blushed there, as well.

And then horror dawned on him, and he barely kept himself from swearing all over again. "You're not, are you?" Just because she'd covered up all that glory of a body with her ugly suits at the office didn't mean she had kept the wonders from her boyfriend.

What had she said his name was?

Mike? Mark?

He realized he was pretty much hating the other guy right about now, which was ludicrous.

Drew didn't do jealousy.

He hadn't when the woman he'd vowed to love until death did them part cheated on him with his best friend, so why the hell was he feeling that way now when he thought about a guy who Deanna had already admitted she was no longer even seeing?

Her lips had pinched together. "No, I'm not a virgin," she said witheringly. "Not that it's any of your business."

"Why the hell not? You know all about my love life."

"That's because you bring it into the office," she exclaimed, her arms flying out to her sides. "And expect me to help you get rid of them when they no longer amuse you."

"I don't do that," he dismissed.

She gave him an "Oh, really?" look that was just as effective as any similar ones he'd gotten from his mother growing up whenever he'd tried to claim innocence over some infraction. He would have run his finger around his too-tight collar if he'd been wearing a shirt. Instead, all he could do was grimace and try not to shift his feet like some damn guilty kid.

"Okay, so I've had you order some pieces of jewelry for me," he allowed.

"Humph. You order so much from Zondervan's that when you asked for this—" she held up her hand and wiggled the ring on her finger "—they jumped to help you out!"

"So?" His voice tightened defensively. "At least I don't have my assistant break up with the girls I date! I'm not that big a crumb."

She exhaled noisily, the fight seeming to go out of her in one big rush. "You're not a crumb." She sat back down again on the bed. She gave him a sidelong look, and actually managed to stay sitting there, though she did rearrange the edges of the towel to cover her knees.

He considered telling her that it was too late for her to bother covering much of anything now that he'd seen it all.

In glorious, God-given, high-definition detail.

Maybe he should be running Hades instead of just moving in. It might suit him better even than running Fortune Forecasting.

Drew Fortune, vice president of hellfire and damnation.

"It's just the situation," she said, drawing him back to terra firma. "It's making me a little—or a lot—crazy."

He would have sat down beside her, but common sense warned him it would be better all around if he didn't.

And because his common sense felt in dangerously short supply, he figured he'd better pay attention when it did rear its head.

"It's only for a few days," he assured, speaking to himself as much as to her. "Then we'll go back home and things can get back to normal."

"Until we have to come up with a wedding and move in together," she countered in a low voice. "What if people ask if we've set a wedding date? What are we supposed to tell them, then?"

"We'll tell them we're still deciding on a date. Hell, we'll tell them we're planning a quick trip to Vegas. I don't know, all right? We'll think of something."

She gave him a quick, narrow look. "You're not breaking out into a rash or anything are you? I mean, we are tossing around the terms marriage and wedding quite a bit here."

"Smart aleck." But at least she'd recovered her equanimity enough to razz him about it.

That at least was something they were both comfortable with. He teased her about being completely anal when it came to details around the office and she gave him heck about everything else.

It was the constant in their relationship.

And now, now he'd had to go and remember what he'd spent nearly four years trying to forget.

That Deanna Gurney wasn't just a stellar assistant.

She was a desirable woman.

And as far as everyone else in Red Rock was concerned, she was ostensibly his woman.

It was ironic as anything in life could be that she was even more off-limits than she'd ever been, thanks to the agreement they'd struck.

Not only could he still remember how it had felt to kiss her four years ago, but now he had the Technicolor image of her body indelibly etched in his head, and his skin still felt singed from the heat of her body in his arms.

"We'll work things out," he finally said.

She was looking down at her hands, spread flat on her lap. "Promise?"

"I do. Promise, that is." He smiled crookedly when she looked at him and was glad to see the small one she gave him in return. "Drink your coffee if it's not gone cold," he urged. "I don't know what Isabella puts in it, but it's pretty good."

She pressed her lips together for a moment. "Okay."

"And I'll go find something to do for thirty minutes. Is that enough time for you to finish dressing?"

At that, her smile did widen. Wryly. "Five minutes would do."

In his experience, he hadn't met a woman who could dress that quickly.

Undress, sure.

His gaze kept straying to the hollow at the base of her throat. He'd never realized before just how sexy that spot was…

"Drew?"

He shook off the haze that encroached on him way too easily and reached behind him for the door. "Fifteen minutes, then. After I shower and change, we'll probably have to head off for the church, but you can still grab some food from the kitchen while I'm getting ready. There was stuff left after I ate, and I know Isabella is looking forward to meeting you."

Which just had her looking worried all over again.

"Don't worry. There're all gonna love you," he assured. And before he could say anything else that would either worry her more or set them back on the sex track where they had no business running, he let himself out of the room and closed the door.

The sooner they got through his father's wedding and the next few days and they could get back to San Diego and some normalcy, the better.

"So there's the newly engaged!"

The loud greeting was called across the expanse of lawn between the crowded parking lot and the church when they arrived nearly two hours later.

Deanna felt Drew's hand tighten around hers as they crossed the grass leading up to a lovely, old-fashioned-looking church. It was white with a tall steeple, and outside, the building was surrounded by an expanse of emerald-green lawn and lush greenery dotted with pink and red flowers. There were garlands of green and white wound around the railings of shallow steps leading up to the wooden double doors, which were bedecked with wreaths of even more flowers.

And for the first time since the debacles of the morning, she was able to forget everything but that moment.

Mostly.

The feel of Drew's hand wrapped around hers wouldn't let her completely forget.

Still, the sight of the church was like something out of a magazine. Or a fantasy. "It's beautiful," she breathed.

"Too bad it'll be the sight of Dad's worst mistake," Drew said in a low tone.

"Judging by the happy looks I'm seeing on people's faces, they don't share your view," Deanna pointed out, just as low. "Just promise me you won't stand up and shoot off a flare gun when the minister asks if there's anyone present who objects."

They'd driven into town by themselves, using one of the trucks from Molly's Pride and judging by the scarcity of available parking spots and the number of people milling around on the grass outside the church, they weren't exactly beating any early arrival records.

Not surprising, given Drew's continuing displeasure with the entire affair.

"That's Nick," he told her as he lifted his free hand in a wave toward the guy who'd called out the greeting.

She would have guessed that, from the description that Drew had given her of his brothers. Nick was about the same height as Drew, although a little more leanly built. But he had the same brown hair and as they got closer, she realized, the same brown eyes. More specifically, though, it was the pretty redhead who stood beside him with a baby on the hip of her narrow blue sheath dress that helped identify him.

"And Darr, presumably, is standing beside him?"

"Yeah."

The youngest Fortune brother was not quite as tall as Nick, but he was stocky and muscular. He was also wearing a string tie with his blinding-white shirt and dark suit, while his brothers wore traditional ones with theirs, and he had a cowboy hat on his head.

Drew had told her that Darr was the most "Texan" of the Fortune transplants to Red Rock, and the seriously good-looking man was definitely living up to that. Particularly when he doffed his hat once she and Drew stopped in front of him and greeted her with a "ma'am," an up-and-down look that told her he was taking her measure and a grin that she hoped meant he wasn't entirely disappointed with the results.

She shouldn't care so much whether Drew's family liked her, but she did, and hoped her smile was not as shaky as it felt when they reached the group. All eyes seemed to turn toward her as Drew began naming off the players before lifting her hand that he was holding. "And this is Deanna Gurney."

"Your fiancée. That news made it around the family by the time the sun came up this morning." Bethany, the petite blue-eyed blonde holding Darr's hand, gave her a dimpled smile.

"Thank God we had time to get over the shock," Nick drawled, giving Deanna a quick, charming wink, and everyone laughed.

"Oh, you." Bethany shushed him with a wiggle of her fingers as she turned to Deanna and caught her unaware in a quick hug. "We're all just so happy for you." She stepped back and her eyes twinkled. She could have been made from spun sugar, she had such a sweet face. "You look radiant. I love that shade of pink on you. I can never get away with anything darker than this." She dashed her hand over her soft pink dress. "I just look all washed out."

Deanna managed to get out a "Thank you." She thought that "neon" might be more appropriate than "radiant" given the vivid color of her dress, but it was the only compliment she'd received since she'd put it on. Drew had only given her a sort of stunned look when he'd joined her in the great room after he was finished getting ready himself.

Because she'd been a little busy trying not to swallow her tongue at the sight of him in his perfectly tailored black suit, white shirt and pale gray tie with his hair ruthlessly combed back from his handsome face, she had just quickly set aside the hot tea that she'd made for herself and pointed out the keys that J.R. had left behind for them, and they were off.

Bethany had turned to Drew, pulling his head down to plant a kiss on his cheek. "But you're a rascal, Andrew. You had me convinced that you were positively allergic to marriage!"

Deanna's gaze collided with his over his sister-in-law's softly waving hair and she hoped that she was the only one who saw the irony in his eyes. "What can I say?" He patted Bethany's shoulder as she stepped back to make

room for Charlene—Nick's red-haired wife—
and her similar greeting.

Drew gently chucked the baby Charlene
was holding under the chin, earning a chor-
tling giggle, and Deanna barely managed not
to stare.

For some reason, she'd never thought what
Drew would be like around little ones, but to
watch him now, he seemed much more natural than she'd have expected.

He looked at Bethany. "And where's your
munchkin?"

"She's off with Josh. You get Randi anywhere within ten feet of Brandon and Maribel and she wants nothing more to do with her
own mama and daddy."

Bethany turned to Deanna again. "Randi
is actually Miranda. Our two-year-old. But
she moves so fast these days, we started
shortening up her name." She grinned. "And
Brandon is Josh's little boy. He's—Josh, that
is—is Frannie's oldest and Maribel is Frannie's youngest."

Even though Deanna had tried to get a
primer on the family names from Drew, she
still felt lost.

"Frannie's one of my cousins," Drew provided, evidently recognizing her failure to

keep up. "Josh is her son. Frannie and her husband, Roberto Mendoza, have been helping Josh raise Brandon."

"Ah." She nodded, managing to follow the branches of the family tree her mind was drawing. "Mendoza? Isn't that Isabella's—"

"Yeah. They're distant cousins. And those are the rest of the Fortune cousins over there. Frannie's brothers." He pointed toward a trio of men and a woman standing near the steps leading up to the church doors. "The guy leaning against the railing is Ross. He's Aunt Cindy's oldest. He's the P.I. I told you about, and the brunette with him is his wife, Julie. They got married a year ago. Cooper's next. Brown hair, no hat. He's worked on ranches all around the U.S. pretty much, but doesn't spend a helluva lot of time here. So I understand anyway. And then there's Flint. Black hat. Has a spread in upstate New York. And, I don't see Frannie anywhere around." He slid his arm so casually around Deanna's shoulder that she almost didn't startle. "She's the youngest of them and the only girl," he added.

"You talking about Frannie? I just saw her inside with Lily," Jeremy provided, walking up to them.

Deanna had already met him at J.R.'s while

Drew had been getting ready and had immediately liked the somewhat soft-spoken surgeon. She had the feeling he didn't say anything until he knew exactly what he was talking about.

It was something Deanna practiced herself, and usually succeeded at, except when she was dealing with Drew.

Only then did that particular trait seem to completely desert her.

"Has Dad arrived yet?" Jeremy asked. He shot his cuffs and glanced around, his blond hair gleaming in the sunlight.

"Haven't seen him," Nick provided.

"Maybe he's come to his senses," Drew said.

"Thought you'd have given up on that by now," Darr said, giving Drew and Deanna a pointed look. "Dad's in love with Lily. And she's in love with him. Maybe if you spent more than two days a year around here you'd see that for yourself." He looked down at Bethany when she put a hand on his arm.

"Dad's driving himself over from the hotel," Nick said, his tone calm. "He probably went in the church through the back. J.R.'s in there already. There's a room they quarantine the groom in so he doesn't see his bride before it's time."

Charlene swatted him with her hand. "Quarantine," she chided with a smile. "I love it that William and Lily chose New Year's Day for their wedding. I think it's a perfect way to start their life together. And who could ask for a more beautiful day?" She started to shift little Matthew in her arms, but Nick lifted the tot and held him up to his shoulder.

"You think any day is a perfect day for a wedding," he teased.

Deanna had to bite back a little sigh of envy. The fact that he adored his wife was as plain as the nose on his face. And holding that little baby just added to the appeal. "It is lovely out," she said. "It's warmer than I expected it to be." She'd thought she might be chilly with only the sheer length of fabric that matched her dress wrapped around her shoulders, but the sun was bright in the mildly cloudy sky and there was barely even enough breeze to tickle the floating fabric of her skirt.

"Well, well, cuz." A deep voice came from behind them and Drew and Deanna turned to see Cooper Fortune ambling toward them, a grin on his ruggedly handsome, weathered face. "Ross just told me the news. Guess your claim that once was more than enough didn't stick after all." He swept up Deanna's hand

and pressed a kiss to the back of it. "You sure you know what you're getting yourself into with this guy, little lady?"

Her nerves prickled and she quickly glanced at Drew. She still hadn't forgotten his comment about putting his head in a marriage nose "again" and felt shocked all over again at the evidence that he'd obviously been married at one point.

But all he said was, "Don't try charming my girl." He was grinning at his cousin, either oblivious to or choosing to ignore Deanna's questioning gaze. "Damn, Coop. You get uglier every year."

"Older, too," Coop allowed wryly. He also had what Deanna was coming to think of as the Fortune brown eyes.

"Honey, why don't we go check on the groom?" Bethany looked at Drew. "It's about time for things to be getting started, isn't it?"

"Actually—" Charlene was looking at the delicately jeweled watch on her wrist "—it's a little late." She looked around at the guests milling about. "Honestly, I don't even recognize half the people here. Can you believe the turnout?" She tucked her hand around Nick's arm. "Maybe we should start moving inside. Give people a start."

Thinking that Charlene had the right idea, Deanna took a step after them along with the rest, but Drew slid his hand down her arm from her shoulder—an act that made her shiver beneath her thin wrap—and caught her hand, staying her.

"No hurry," he said.

No hurry for him, he meant, but considering the others who were still easily within earshot, she kept the thought to herself.

But as soon as the others were far enough away, having reached the stone walkway circling the church, she pinned him with a look.

"Once was more than enough?" she repeated. "You have been married before, haven't you. When?"

"Does it matter?"

"Uh…yeah." She wanted to pinch him. "If I had a former spouse around somewhere don't you think it'd be odd if I hadn't mentioned him to you, particularly now?" She held up her hand and nudged the diamond ring with her thumb. "What was her name? What happened?"

He grimaced. "Paula. It was right after college. And it lasted for the sum total of three months."

Even though she'd been prepared, she still

felt stunned hearing him confirm that he had
been married before. Her mouth suddenly
felt like she was sucking on a lemon. "Three
months. The usual expiration date. Have you
ever been with a woman longer than that before tiring of her?"

"Other way around." His voice went flat.
"She tired of me."

"Who on earth would get tired of you?" she
exclaimed and promptly felt her face go hot.

"The woman I married, obviously, which
was made very plain to me when I found her
getting busy in our bed with my best friend."

She was floored. "You're serious."

His jaw canted to one side for a moment before centering again. "Unfortunately."

A wave of sympathy plowed over her for
the young man he'd been. "And you were just
out of college. How awful for you."

He just grimaced and looked as if he wished
she'd drop the matter altogether.

"And your family obviously knows what
happened. I can't believe your cousin was in-
sensitive enough to bring it up like that."

"All they know is that it didn't work out."

She stared. "You…didn't tell them why?"

"And prove what a miserable judge of
women I was?"

"Drew…"

"It's ancient history." His voice was short. "I was briefly married. It didn't work out. End of story."

"But it's not." She moved into his path when he took a step toward the church. "You know, ever since we arrived in Red Rock, I've been trying to figure out what instilled such a vehement dislike of marriage in you. I'd always just assumed it had something to do with your growing up—trouble between your mom and dad or something—but then I met J.R. and it's obvious that there's no tension between any of you. And aside from Jeremy—who hasn't said much of anything about the wedding—you're the only one here who isn't openly happy for your father. But now it all makes sense. She broke your heart."

He smoothed down his tie. "Don't start painting a sentimental glaze over it."

Her stomach tensed. "Do you still love her?"

"Hell, no." His voice rose and he glanced around, but nobody was paying them any heed. Everyone was still focused on filing through the opened double doors of the church.

But then his eyes narrowed and Deanna turned to see what had garnered his attention. All she could see was the crowd of people.

But then she realized that one woman in particular was making her way out of the church. She was dressed in a silvery-blue dress that even from several yards away, Deanna could see suited the breathtakingly beautiful woman.

"What's Frannie doing?" Drew mused.

So that was the other cousin. Deanna realized she shouldn't be surprised at the woman's magazine-perfect looks. To a one, all the Fortune men that she'd met had received ample blessings from the genetic pool of good looks.

"I'd say she's looking for someone," Deanna guessed and quickly fell into step when Drew headed toward Frannie.

When they neared, she realized that the cheerful noise of the guests as they'd collected had muted into hushed whispers and furtive glances.

Drew's hand caught hers in a tight grip. He, too, had noticed the mood shift.

They made their way through the people and joined Nick and Darr and their wives who'd joined Frannie.

"What's wrong?" Drew asked.

Frannie looked at him. Her eyes were plainly worried. "We can't find William."

Chapter 6

Three hours later, the groom was still missing.

All the guests had departed, but the family members were still inside the church, either pacing between the pews that were bedecked with clusters of hydrangeas and white roses that matched the enormous sprays decorating the chancel, or sitting in them.

In the rear of the church where the double doors had been closed against the afternoon as well as the departed guests, Bethany was sitting on the floor, her lovely dress spread around her crossed legs as she held Charlene and Nick's baby in her lap and rolled a ball back and forth to her little Randi, keeping the active toddler more or less content.

At the front of the church where she ought to have stood with Drew's father exchanging their marriage vows, Lily was pacing, her long hands twisting together around the cell phone she was clutching.

Every few minutes for the past few hours, she'd held up the small phone and peered at it or dialed it, and every few minutes later, she'd clutch it at her waist again, and pace some more.

She wore high, caramel-tinted ivory pumps that added even more height to her long-limbed figure, and with her dark, sultry features she looked much younger than the sixty-five that Deanna knew her to be. Her dark hair was pinned into a twist with tiny roses at the back of her head that were matched in style with the rose-patterned embroidered lace that covered her bodice and worked its way down into points over the full, wide tea-length skirt. It would have looked like a party dress right out of the '50s except for the color—cream with a hint of coffee added to it—that seemed to add a thoroughly modern edge.

Despite the woman's obvious strain, Deanna could hardly tear her gaze from Lily. She looked elegant and stylish and so lovely that it was heartbreaking to know her groom had seemingly disappeared from the face of the planet.

And then a side door opened and Lily whirled.

Her expression fell, though, when it was Darr and Drew who entered the sanctuary.

"I've checked with the police," Darr said without preamble. "There's been no report of accidents in the vicinity of Red Rock. Closest thing was a single car accident a good seventy miles out, on the highway heading toward Haggarty."

Lily paled but Darr lifted his hand. "There was only one person involved, a woman." He looked solemn. "She didn't make it, but that has nothing to do with Dad, Lily. There've been no emergency calls out of Red Rock, and no incidents between here and San Antonio. I've got some friends at the firehouse who've promised to recheck all the hospitals in a few hours." He shook his head. "Drew checked the hotel where Dad was staying."

Drew sat on the edge of front pew next to Deanna. "His suitcase was packed and sitting on his bed like he was ready to put it in his car," he told them. "But nobody who works there remembers seeing him leave this morning and he definitely didn't check out."

"Lily, why don't you sit down," Isabella suggested softly, stepping into Lily's path to stop her pacing for at least a moment. Like Lily, Isabella had a river of dark brown hair, though hers was a straight sheet down the back of her vibrant, red dress. Deanna was glad to see that Isabella gently maneuvered the cell phone out of Lily's hand.

She might have surrendered the fruitless device, but the older woman just shook her head and continued pacing. "Something has happened," she fretted. "I know William. He was looking forward to this day as much as I was. He could be sick somewhere or..." She shook her head again, her voice trailing off.

Deanna slid a glance toward Drew beside her, but he didn't comment. His thoughts looked far away.

"Of course he was looking forward to being your husband," Isabella soothed. "It's practically all he's talked about for the past few years. We'll figure everything out soon." Her head lifted when J.R. came through the same door that Drew had used. J.R. had driven out to the Double Crown where the wedding reception was to have been held to see personally if there'd been any news there. William had already moved in with Lily, though he'd evidently checked into a hotel to observe the propriety of not seeing his bride on the day before the ceremony.

But J.R. just shook his head. "I told the caterer they could go ahead and pack up." He eyed Lily. "I didn't think you needed to have to deal with that, too."

"Thank you, dear." Lily turned to face the simple wooden cross that hung above the chancel area. Her shoulders slowly lifted and fell. "Ever since I lost Ryan I've felt that he's been there, still watching out for us all." Lily's voice was husky. "I have to still believe that."

Deanna blinked hard and looked away.

But a moment later, the bride had turned around to face them. Her expression was drawn, but her chin was lifted. "I do still believe that. But there's no purpose to hanging around here." She stepped down the three shallow steps leading up to the chancel and her beautiful gown swayed slightly around her shapely ankles. "The caterer won't take away the food. So if anyone is hungry, they should come out to the Double Crown. Nothing will be solved by any of us collapsing from hunger." She looked toward Isabella. "Would you be so kind and let the reverend know we're finally getting out of the way so the custodian and groundskeeper can clean up around here? I know they still need to prepare for regular services tomorrow." She cradled her hand around the spray of flowers decorating the end of the pew were Deanna and Drew were sitting. "If any of you want some flowers, take them. They're too lovely to waste."

Not surprisingly, nobody seemed inclined to enjoy the flowers now, beautiful or not.

Drew pushed to his feet beside her. "Has anyone considered the notion that something else might have happened to Dad?"

Deanna sucked in a breath. "Drew—" He surely wouldn't offer the suggestion that William had changed his mind, would he?

He shook his head sharply, though, and she fell silent. She hadn't seen such an expression on his face since the morning she'd gotten to the office early and found him sitting at his desk with an empty bottle of whiskey beside him, looking at a photograph of his mother.

"He's a Fortune," Drew continued. "We can't allow ourselves to forget that fact."

J.R. folded his arms across his wide chest. Like his brothers, he too had discarded his suit coat and rolled the sleeves of his dress shirt up his forearms. "What are you thinking?"

"I don't know. But we all know it wouldn't be the first time someone's deliberately brought harm to this family."

Deanna gasped. "No." But she saw the way Lily's hand jerked, then moved away from the hydrangea blossom and the petals that rained down onto the carpet after. She quickly slid her arm around the woman's slender waist and nudged her toward the pew. "Sit. Please."

Lily sat. She pressed her fist against her chest. "Nobody would want to harm William," she said, but there was a fresh shimmer of fear in her voice.

"Maybe not," Darr allowed and Deanna saw the look he and Drew exchanged. "But this family *has* had more than a few incidences."

"What about kidnapping?" Drew looked toward Nick and J.R. He hated being the one to voice the possibility, but he already knew that he and Darr were on the same page.

"Dear Lord," Isabella whispered. She, too, sat, then suddenly leaned her head forward until it touched her knees.

"Honey?" J.R. started.

But she just lifted a hand, waving at him. "I'm fine. I just got dizzy for a minute."

Frowning, J.R. sat next to her, his hand resting on her back.

"We're all getting ahead of ourselves." The voice of reason came, surprisingly, from the cotton candy-soft-looking Bethany who walked up the aisle with her miniature version toddling after her.

Charlene brought up the rear, holding her sleeping baby. "She's right. Imagining outlandish scenarios isn't helping the situation."

"It's not outlandish, though," Lily countered shakily.

Isabella had sat up again. Her face was pale. "The fires a few years ago. First at Jose and Maria's restaurant and then the one at your barn."

Lily was nodding.

"But Lloyd Fredericks is dead, Lyndsey Pollack is locked safely away in a psychiatric facility and her mother's still rotting in jail," Nick pointed out. His tone was reasonable, but Deanna—feeling more lost than ever—could see that his expression, too, had taken on a new worry.

"Well, if it is a kidnapping," Bethany said, "then someone ought to be at the Double Crown in case they try contacting Lily, right?"

She grimaced. "One thing I've learned from having a father who owns the largest private oil company in Texas is what to expect in situations like his. My father was always fearful that my brother and sister and I would end up being targets for people like that."

"Bethany is right." Lily pushed to her feet. She was still pale, but at least she looked steadier. And resolved. "I want to go back to the ranch no matter what."

"We'll drive you," J.R. immediately offered.

"Thank you, dear."

Isabella stood, too, and smoothed down her dress. "I'll speak with the reverend first and meet you out front."

Lily nodded and took J.R.'s arm when he offered it and they all began recessing out of the church. But it was as far as it could get from the recessional they'd all expected when they'd started out that day.

The air had taken on a strong chill when they left through the front doors, gray clouds gathering where only hours ago there had been pretty white puffs of clouds and sunshine.

It was horribly fitting and Deanna shivered.

"Here." Drew slid his suit coat over the thin wrap around her shoulders.

"Thanks." She clutched it around herself. The scent of him that clung to the fabric was even more comforting than the warmth. Then Isabella joined them and everyone silently aimed across the grass for the parking lot.

It looked desolate, compared to how crowded it had been earlier that day.

No one noticed the person standing in the lengthening shadow cast by the church, a large push broom in hand, watching them climb into their trucks and cars and slowly drive away from the church.

When they were gone, the groundskeeper turned and eyed the pile of flower petals and other bits of debris that the broom had collected from the back of the church. Only one of the Fortunes would have thought to decorate the rear door of the church that was only ever used by staff.

But it really wasn't the pile of trash that had the groundskeeper's full attention.

It was the tiny infant swaddled in a car seat.

The groundskeeper had found the baby sitting next to the rear door more than two hours ago, but even when the guests started streaming out of the church after the wedding that wasn't, nobody came back to claim the kid, even though it had been crying its head off. Eventually, the baby had stopped its thin wails and gone to sleep.

And still no one came to get the baby.

Everyone inside the church was too concerned about the old Fortune guy to bother looking around for a baby who evidently shouldn't have been there in the first place.

Now, the worker crouched down and touched the gold medallion that hung from a thin chain around the baby and blanket. It wasn't a large medallion but against the baby it sure looked that way. It also looked valuable.

"Who do you belong to?"

But the baby just continued sleeping, its little mouth sucking its own lip.

The groundskeeper straightened and finished sweeping up, moving faster because fat raindrops had begun to fall, making the task even more of a pain.

Cleaning up after other people had never really been part of the plan…

Then, after putting the cleaning gear away, the worker returned to pick up the car seat and the baby.

Nobody noticed…or cared…when they disappeared into the evening.

* * *

Drew and Deanna drove back to Molly's Pride in silence.

Everyone else had gone to the Double Crown to be with Lily.

Drew couldn't bring himself to be among them.

Not because of his feelings where Lily was concerned. He'd seen for himself just how devastated she'd been when his father hadn't made it to the church.

But because Drew couldn't get the last, angry words he'd had with William out of his head.

He'd told his father he could go to hell and take his new wife with him, if William really expected Drew to find a freaking wife.

What if his father didn't come back?

What if he couldn't?

"Who are Lloyd Fredericks and Lyndsey Pollack?" Deanna's soft voice finally broke the silence when they went inside his brother's hacienda.

"It's an old story."

"It didn't sound that way back at the church."

His hands tightened at his sides, remembering the turmoil the duo had wrought on the family. He turned toward the center of the house, his shoes echoing hollowly against the distressed floor as his thoughts kept whirling inside his head.

"Lloyd was Frannie's first husband," he finally answered. "Lyndsey was Josh's girlfriend. She was pregnant with Brandon, but her real interest wasn't in making a family with Josh—it was the huge inheritance from Frannie's father that he came into when he turned eighteen."

"Frannie's father being your aunt Cindy's husband," Deanna clarified.

"One of four husbands." He reached the alcove that overlooked the center courtyard and stared out at the open space. Scrolled iron sconces cast pools of light around the courtyard and the sprinkles of rain were increasing, making the tile on the fountain gleam.

He looked at Deanna.

She was still clutching his jacket around herself and her eyes looked huge for her face. Her mother might have some emotional problems to deal with, but he seriously doubted that Deanna had the kind of traumatic events in her family tree that the Fortunes did.

And now, he felt like the worst kind of selfish idiot for not having forewarned her. God only knew what was going on in Red Rock with his father disappearing.

"You should go back to San Diego," he said abruptly.

"What? Now? No way."

"What if things get dangerous?"

Her brows pulled together, a mutinous set to her slightly pointed chin that he'd seen often enough in the past to know she meant business. "What if they do?" she challenged. "Your family believes we're engaged." She waved her hand with the ring, as if he needed reminding. "What kind of a person would I seem like if I cut and ran now?"

"They'd think maybe I was trying to keep you safe!"

She looked bewildered. "From what?"

"Murder. Arson. Take your pick." His voice turned flat. He looked back out at the rain. It was easier than looking at her. Because when he did, all he wanted to do was pull her in his arms and just hang on. "We've had all of that touch our family at one time or another," he finished.

"Good Lord." Her dress rustled as she sat on the edge of one of the deep leather chairs positioned to look out on the courtyard. "Just fill me in, all right? Because my imagination will come up with things probably much worse than what actually has happened."

"Don't count on it." He exhaled.

"What happened with Josh's father?"

"Lloyd, you mean?" He grimaced. "Turned out he wasn't Josh's father at all, but everyone—including Frannie, thanks to her mother's machinations—thought he was." He sat down on the coffee table, still looking out on the courtyard. "In any case, the inheritance that Lyndsey had her eyes on was the same money that Lloyd wanted to get his hands on—one of the reasons why he married Frannie in the first place."

"Sounds like a prince."

"Yeah. I don't think anyone in the family ever much cared for him, except maybe Cindy. She thought he was a great catch for her daughter, whether Frannie agreed or not. Anyway, Lyndsey and her lunatic mother weren't interested in having to compete for Josh's inheritance when it did come through, and they caused all sorts of trouble. They tampered with Cindy's brakes on her car when she was in town trying to make nice with Frannie after all the crap she'd pulled on her, they practically burned down Red—it's a great Mexican place owned by the Mendozas." He glanced at her. "The Fortunes and the Mendozas go way back. Isabella's half brother manages the place now. Anyway, they also tried to torch Lily's barn when she had an event going on there with hundreds of kids. Darr got hurt, actually, trying to save the horses in the barn. Lily still lost one, but nobody but Darr was hurt."

"And he obviously recovered," Deanna observed.

Drew nodded once. The fact that Darr's injuries had healed didn't make up for the fact that the crime had occurred in the first place. "Lloyd eventually ended up dead and Frannie was initially arrested for it. Then Roberto—Josh's real dad and the guy that Frannie's married to now—confessed to the murder. They were both just trying to protect Josh, who they feared might have done it. But ultimately, it turned out that Lyndsey and her mother had been behind all of the violence all along."

"How horrible for them all. And that poor little baby." She moved from the chair to the coffee table beside him, slipping his jacket off her shoulders to rest across her lap.

The useless strip of thin fabric she'd had wrapped around her shoulders at the church had slid down, exposing the silky-looking expanse of her shoulders.

He focused on the hardwood floor. It was old. It was scuffed and nicked.

And it gleamed with an unexpected, shining warmth.

So did Deanna's sun-kissed, bare shoulders.

He closed his eyes for a moment.

What the hell was wrong with him?

His father had gone missing, for Christ's sake.

He cleared his throat, too aware of the silent house breathing around them. "Wouldn't worry about Brandon much. He's in good hands now. Frannie and Roberto are helping Josh with him. But they've all had to come to terms with some pretty serious lies from Cindy and Lloyd that opened the door for what ended up happening in the first place. Toss in psychotic Lyndsey and it was a recipe for disaster."

Deanna let out a long breath and shook her head slightly. She put her hand on his arm, squeezing a little before moving it back to her lap. But the zinging warmth of her touch remained. He curled his fist and was damned if he knew if he was trying to hold on to the warmth or get rid of it.

"I thought I had a crazy mother," she was saying. "But the worst thing that Gigi's ever done was get fired for engaging in inappropriate behavior in the workplace."

He gave her a look. "What's that supposed to mean?"

She looked away. "Use your imagination."

He could think of only a few things. Stealing. Doing drugs. Or having sex.

Somehow—maybe it was the way Deanna always was the soul of propriety in the office—he was betting on the last. And he also figured that her mother had done a few other things that weren't so great.

Like spending herself into the poorhouse and expecting her daughter to bail her out.

There was something seriously upside down there.

Not that he was in any position to judge family relationships.

He'd accused his father of forgetting his own family in favor of Lily.

And dammit all to hell, he couldn't stop smelling the green apple scent of his assistant's glossy red hair.

He pushed to his feet again, moving to the window. The glass felt chilly against his palm when he pressed his hand against it. "I'd feel better if you went back."

"Because you don't want me in the way?"

He shot her a look. "Did I say that?"

"No, but that doesn't mean it wasn't what you meant. It's one thing to need a fiancée for appearances' sake at a wedding. It's another thing to have her hanging around where you don't want her when the situation has changed."

He turned toward her, staring. "God help a woman's mind. All I was thinking about is your freaking safety!"

"Well, you don't have to yell at me!"

"I'm not." But his voice was raised. And so was hers.

He turned again and looked out at the courtyard and wished he were standing on the beach. But not even having an ocean spread out in front of him was going to be enough to swallow up the roiling turmoil inside of him.

"Drew." Her voice was soft. She set aside his jacket and stood up, moving beside him. Her fingertips grazed his arm. "Your father is going to be all right."

His jaw tightened until it ached. "None of us know that."

Deanna swallowed past the lump in her throat. She covered his clenched fist with hers. Maybe their engagement wasn't rooted in the normal things, but that didn't mean she didn't genuinely care about him. "I'm not leaving until we do."

He turned and closed his hands around her shoulders. "What if something happens to you?"

She swallowed the shiver that had absolutely nothing to do with some imagined fear on his part and everything to do with him. "Nothing is going to happen. And I am not leaving."

"I could fire you."

She met his gaze head-on. "You won't."

"I could tell everyone that we broke up."

Her jaw tightened. "You could."

"They'd figure it was my fault, that I was just acting true to form. Blowing through women. Nobody would think less of you for deserting me during a crisis."

"I think you're underestimating your family's opinion of you."

"You've been here less than twenty-four hours and you've come to that conclusion, have you?"

Deanna almost could have smiled if the situation weren't so serious. "It doesn't take a genius to recognize how much you all care for each other." The fact that she didn't have those family relationships made it particularly obvious to her. "And we could debate this for the rest of the evening, or you can just accept the fact that I am not leaving you."

His brows pulled together. She could see the argument he still wanted to make in his stance. Could feel it in the fingers he was pressing into her shoulders.

"Why?"

There it was again. Just Drew. Plain and simple and wholly devastating and he made her mouth run dry.

But he was waiting for an answer and just then, she didn't have the strength—or even the desire—to prevaricate. So she swallowed past the dryness and told the truth. "Two weeks after I started working for you, I came into the office early one morning. To prep for an important meeting. Nobody should have been there yet. But the light was on in your office." She watched his jaw tighten. Shift slightly to one side before centering again. "You were—"

"—passed out," he said flatly.

"—asleep at your desk," she softened the truth, because his all-night bender wasn't really her point. "You'd been there all night." His mother's funeral had been only days before.

"You dragged me up and pulled me together for the biggest meeting of my career."

"I fixed you coffee and found a clean shirt and tie for you."

"And I paid you back by trying to jump your bones."

Her cheeks felt like they were on fire. "You kissed me," she corrected moderately.

"But you didn't walk, didn't sue. You could have done both."

"I believed you when you said it wouldn't happen again." He'd made that point abundantly clear. And in the years since, she'd recognized why. She simply was not the type of woman he was attracted to, which also wasn't her point.

Although even thinking about that long-ago morning was as much a double-edged sword as it ever was.

"But what made me stay," she finished quietly, "was the look in your eyes that morning."

"Hungover?" His voice turned caustic.

"No. The look that told me you were a man who knew what it meant to honestly, really care—deeply—about someone. I knew then that you were going to be a good man to work with."

"So says the woman who sent my staff home early yesterday because she thought I was being unreasonably demanding."

She drew in a breath. That was the layer of Drew that made him more of a challenge.

"A good man, period," she said. "And I've seen that same look in your eyes ever since your father didn't show up at the church. That's why I didn't quit on you before. And that's why I'm not quitting on you now. I am not leaving."

His eyes narrowed. His hands tightened around her shoulders, drawing her closer to him, until there was not an inch of breath to be had between her body and his. "And what if I kissed you again now?"

He was trying to make her run.

She knew it as surely as she knew her own name.

And even though she felt weak in the knees and shivers were slipping down her spine, she lifted her chin.

Her gaze met his. "What if you did?"

Chapter 7

Drew's lashes narrowed until all Deanna could see was the thin glimmer of golden-brown. Her breath stalled in her throat when his hands slowly slid over her shoulders, to her neck.

He lowered his head. "What if I did?" His thumbs rested at the base of her throat and she became acutely aware of her pulse throbbing there.

His thumbs slowly climbed her throat until they reached the underside of her chin. They nudged it upward.

His lips hovered above hers, so close that if

either one of them moved an inch...less than an inch...they'd meet.

A door suddenly slammed somewhere in the house.

It might as well have been cymbals crashing behind them.

Drew's head lifted.

Deanna jumped back.

"Christ," he muttered, shoveling his hands through his hair.

Deanna scrabbled with her wrap that had fallen to the floor without her even noticing. The thin fabric slithered through her shaking fingers as she picked it up and tried to pull it around her shoulders. It just kept tangling and in the end, she bunched it between her hands.

She couldn't look at Drew.

After the way she'd behaved when she'd wakened that morning, for her to turn around and practically throw herself at him now?

Her entire body felt flushed.

Sadly, she knew it wasn't exactly embarrassment, either.

If he really would have kissed her...

"Oh, there you are." Isabella appeared in the doorway. "I knew you had to be around somewhere because the truck was out front." She brushed aside a long lock of dark hair from her pale cheek. "I don't suppose you've heard any—no. Of course you haven't, or you would have let us know." Thankfully, as Isabella settled on the arm of the same chair that Deanna had used what seemed only moments ago, Isabella didn't seem to notice the air that—to Deanna—felt as thick as molasses. "Seems fitting that this rain came out of nowhere, doesn't it?" She shook her dark head and sighed. "J.R. is staying out with Lily for a while. Jeremy came back with me, though. He said he had some calls to return." Her lips stretched into a humorless smile. "I guess when you're in medicine you're not allowed to get completely away from emergencies even when you're having one of your own."

Deanna made a faint sound of agreement. She could see Drew in her periphery, standing like a stone monolith in front of the windows. "How...how was Lily?"

"Out of her mind. And holding herself together with as much dignity as she always does." Isabella ran her hands down her red dress. "I don't know how she does it, if it's just practice after having lost Ryan as suddenly as she did or what. Not that William is lost," she added rapidly. "We don't know that at all."

"Yet." Drew's voice was dark.

Deanna bit her lip. Their hostess looked nearly as upset as Drew sounded with a pallor under her smooth complexion that clearly showed her strain. "Isabella, why don't you and Drew try to relax a little. I could fix you something to eat. Jeremy may need something, too." Deanna didn't have any idea if either Isabella or Jeremy had eaten something out at the Double Crown, but if they hadn't, then it had been hours since they'd had breakfast before they'd gone to the church.

"Eat." Isabella shook her head and pushed herself off the arm of the chair. "My brain is just not tracking today. That's why I came back. Evie left after breakfast for a few weeks of vacation and I knew you all would be hungry by now. Lily was right about her caterers leaving a ton of food, but all we did was pack it up and store it in the freezer. Nobody was in the mood to have wedding reception food, you know?"

"I can imagine. You look exhausted, though. You shouldn't be worrying about feeding us," Deanna assured quickly. She'd forgotten all about Isabella and J.R.'s housekeeper, Evie. She'd only met her in passing when she'd made herself tea while waiting for Drew to get dressed for the wedding. "If you don't mind me intruding in your kitchen, I'm happy to put something together." She'd seen for herself that the large kitchen was amply stocked.

And truthfully, Deanna wanted something—anything—that she could turn her attention to.

The other woman tucked her hair behind her ear. "You're practically family, Deanna. There's no intruding at all. We'll both do it. It won't be hard. Evie's left us with a ton of food. I think she's afraid J.R. and I might starve in her absence." She glanced at Drew. "Is there anything I can get you right now, Drew? Coffee? Beer?"

He shook his head and finally moved away from the windows. "I need to talk to Jeremy," he said and brushed past Deanna as he strode out of the room.

Deanna's hands strangled the balled-up fabric as her gaze followed him.

"Poor man," Isabella murmured after a moment. "This has to be making him as crazy as it is J.R. and the others." She tucked her hand through Deanna's arm as they left the alcove. "We're all so glad that you're here with him. That he's not alone."

Deanna managed a weak smile. "I'm glad I'm here, too." That, at least, was the absolute truth. "Do you and J.R. get to see a lot of Mr. Fortune?"

"William," Isabella corrected with a gentle smile. "He's going to be your father-in-law, remember? I refuse to think otherwise."

Deanna knew what Isabella meant, but she still felt her face flushing all over again.

Fortunately, they'd reached the spacious kitchen and Isabella let go of Deanna's arm and headed toward the wide refrigerator. "And to answer your question, yes, we see William and Lily quite a bit. For one thing, Lily is a natural hostess. She always has something going on out at the Double Crown." She turned with a large chunk of cheese in her hand and set it on the center island. "Jeremy's probably going to tell Drew. We had the radio on during the drive here from Lily's. The news outlets have already gotten hold of the story."

"Mr. Fortune—William—is a prominent businessman." Deanna set her crumpled scarf on a bar stool. "I can't say that I'm really surprised at that." She bit her lip. If she hadn't been so concerned with Drew, she would have foreseen the matter herself. "Drew should issue an official statement on behalf of Fortune Forecasting." And how awful it was going to be to carefully craft that statement when they knew so little.

"That's what Jeremy said." Isabella set two enormous, red tomatoes next to the cheese. "What was unexpected though, was they speculated that William wanted to disappear. Not just skip out on his wedding, but skip out on his life. They were even referring to things in his life that happened more than forty years ago. Business failures, that sort of thing."

Deanna stared. "But that's ridiculous."

"You know that. I know that. Everyone in the family—" Isabella waved her hand around "—everyone who knows William knows that. But there are people who don't, and people who love to gossip and make up things out of the clear blue sky." She pulled a knife out of a drawer. "And we're the ones who have to hear such nonsense." She shook her head, her lips twisting. "As if this isn't hard enough to deal with."

"I don't know what to say. Try not to think about it?" Deanna smiled weakly.

But the other woman tilted her head and nodded. "You're right, actually. Focus on the positive." Her eyes focused again on Deanna. "So that's what we'll do. I meant to tell you earlier. That dress is beautiful on you."

"That wasn't exactly what I meant," Deanna managed wryly. But if talking about clothes helped keep the worry out of Isabella's eyes, she was game. "But I really never thought this dress suited me at all. I kind of packed in a hurry."

"The color's spectacular with your hair. And if my shoulders and arms were as toned as yours, I'd wear halters, too. You should either change or put on an apron, though."

Deanna lifted her eyebrows. "You're as dressed up as I am, Isabella," she reminded gently.

"Right." The other woman shook her head again, as if she were clearing it of cobwebs. "My brain today. We'll both change. Meet you back here." She set her knife down with a clatter.

Deanna nodded and they headed to their respective bedrooms and her feet slowed as she passed the closed door to Jeremy's room. She could hear the murmur of voices behind the door and took an easier breath. Drew was obviously still talking with his brother.

She let out a long breath and made herself move on. When she reached the bedroom they were sharing, she quickly pulled out her jeans and a sweater before reaching back to unfasten the tiny dress hook behind her neck. But when she caught her reflection in the oversize mirror leaning against the wall, she paused.

Maybe the fact that Gigi had given her the dress had colored her opinion about it.

Her gaze strayed to the chest of drawers where her purse was sitting. Her phone was inside it, still turned off. Heaven only knew how many messages from Gigi were waiting.

What was wrong with Deanna that even now, considering the way all of the Fortunes were frantic with concern over their parent, she still couldn't bring herself to turn on that phone and speak with her own very alive-and-well mother?

She wasn't even sure if her reluctance made her feel guilty or not.

"You're a horrible daughter," she whispered to her reflection. It was a frequent refrain, although before that week when Deanna had finally taken a stand with her mother, it was a refrain that had always been sung strictly by Gigi.

She sighed and removed the dress, hanging it on one of the hangers in the closet. Then she changed into the comfort zone provided by her well-worn jeans and the faded green sweater that she'd knitted for herself during high school Home Ec and went back out to the kitchen.

Isabella was already there. She, too, had changed into soft-looking jeans and a sweater.

But what sent Deanna's heart plunging through her stomach was the sight of the other woman sitting on the bar stool, her head bent forward over her knees.

"Isabella?" She rushed into the kitchen. "Is there news?"

Isabella lifted her hand, but not her head. "It's okay." Her voice was muffled. "It's not William. Just give me a second."

Deanna leaned against the island, letting her panic subside until she could breath. She frowned at the woman's downturned head, then went to the cupboards near the sink, opening and closing doors until she found a glass. She filled it with water and took it over to Isabella.

She crouched down on her heels so she could see Isabella's face beneath her thick curtain of hair. "You got dizzy again, didn't you?" she guessed. "Like you did at the church."

Isabella opened her eyes, sliding a guilty look her way before slowly sitting up. Her curtain of dark hair slid down behind her back as she nodded.

"Drink some water." Deanna fit the glass into Isabella's hand, prepared to catch it if she wasn't able to hold on to it. "Are you feeling sick?"

Isabella lifted the glass and drank down half the contents. Then she let out a long breath. "I think I might be pregnant," she said in a low voice.

Deanna's lips parted. "That sounds…wonderful…doesn't it?"

Isabella's lips turned up at the corners. "Absolutely. It just seems like now isn't exactly the time to add that to everyone's plate." Her glance slipped past Deanna toward the empty doorway as she set the glass on the counter. "J.R. and I didn't tell anyone at the time, but I had a miscarriage about six months ago."

"Oh, Isabella…"

The other woman raised her hand. "It's all right. And we weren't really trying to keep it a secret or anything. It was a blow, of course, once we realized, but I was so early along, I didn't even know I'd been pregnant until the doctor told me. I just don't want J.R. worrying about this right now."

"Not that I have even twenty-four hours to base this on," Deanna offered, "but I'm pretty sure he would want to be worrying about you. He's clearly devoted to you."

Isabella smiled. The color was coming back into her cheeks, much to Deanna's relief. "And I am to him," she assured. She slid off the bar stool and went around the island again to pick up the knife she'd left there. "We've wanted to start a family ever since we got married two years ago. I know J.R. will be thrilled. And I know he'll be worried whether he admits it or not. I'm already thirty-two. Like it or not, this sort of thing just seems to get more complicated with every year past thirty. And I don't know for certain, yet. I haven't done a test. It's just a hunch. Not only do I not want him worrying more just now, but I also don't want to raise his hopes if I'm wrong." She deftly sliced a tomato in half. "You can understand that, right?"

Deanna nodded. "Yes." She lifted her hands. "But what can I do to help?" She meant more than just the dinner preparation, and the other woman knew it.

"You're the only one I've told," Isabella said. She let out a deep breath. "Just being able to tell someone is a lot, believe me." She reached below the island and pulled out a cheese grater and a plastic bowl and set them on the counter. "And you can grate."

Deanna knew that the other woman would never have shared her suspicion if she didn't believe Deanna and Drew were heading toward the altar, and her conscience weighed heavily.

But she nodded and moved around the island to stand beside the other woman, and began unwrapping the cheese. "You'll let me know if you do need something, all right? Even if it's just to sneak a pregnancy test into the house for you."

Isabella laughed softly. "I knew I liked you, Dee."

And Deanna liked Isabella.

She liked every member of Drew's family that she'd met since arriving in Red Rock.

And she hated the deception that she and Drew had created.

But she hated the thought of letting him down more.

They ate their late supper of salad and spicy enchiladas and chased it down with the most delicious caramel cake that Deanna had ever tasted in her life. But she strongly suspected that the only reason Jeremy and Drew did any justice to the meal was because they didn't want to disappoint Isabella.

Then, while they were eating the decadent dessert that Evie had left for them, J.R. returned. Lily had finally gone to bed, he reported, primarily because William's brother Patrick and his wife, Lacey, had come to the Double Crown and Lacey had been able to convince her cousin-in-law that she simply had to get some rest.

"Would she take a sedative?" Jeremy asked.

"I doubt it," Isabella cautioned.

"Given the state she was in, let's hope that doesn't become necessary," J.R. told him.

"Is anyone staying with her?" Deanna asked.

"Lacey," J.R. said. "For tonight at least. She and Patrick have a brief trip they're leaving on tomorrow that they can't postpone." J.R. leaned back in his seat at the head of the table. Isabella sat adjacent to him and their hands were linked on top of the table. "I don't think any of us want her to be alone right now. Fortunately, there are enough family members around town that we can keep that duty covered without too much effort."

"I could go tomorrow," Isabella offered immediately.

J.R. eyed her. "You look more tired than I feel," he said. "Frannie's already said she'll go over tomorrow. You can all work out details then."

Deanna quickly focused on the bright yellow-and-orange linen napkin on her lap, folding it in fourths. If Isabella was right, she had a good reason to look tired right now.

"Lily doesn't look like the type to appreciate being babysat."

They all turned to look at Drew. He hadn't said a word at the table to anyone other than Deanna sitting beside him, when he'd told her they'd craft a media release before morning.

"She's not," Isabella agreed after a moment. "She'd hate feeling coddled. But right now, I know she's more focused on William than she is on herself." She stood and began reaching for plates.

Deanna rose to help. She was more than a little surprised when the others did, too. Even Drew.

Since the man didn't even order his own lunch at the office if he could avoid it, she wasn't exactly used to seeing him carrying dirty dishes anywhere, much less to the kitchen sink, where he began rinsing them, as well as the others that were quickly stacked beside him before J.R. disappeared to take care of some ranch matters and Jeremy went off to return yet another call from his service.

"I'll finish up in here," Deanna offered to Isabella, who looked ready to shoo Drew out of the way, and was relieved when the other woman accepted, even subsiding to her husband's none-too-subtle efforts before he'd left that she retire for the night.

"Tomorrow is going to be a better day," she said before she left the kitchen.

Which left Deanna alone in the room with Drew.

And the last time they'd been alone—

She cut off the treacherous thoughts.

It was harder than it should have been, though, and only by mentally pulling on one of her ugly suits as a paltry armor against the feelings inside her did she find the strength to move naturally next to him as if she hadn't thrown herself at him the way she had.

But her gaze still kept straying to his sinewy forearms below the rolled-up sleeves of his white shirt. "I can do that," she told him a little more abruptly than her "act natural" act called for.

"So can I." He stuck a plate under the running water and rinsed it. Water sluiced over his bronzed wrist. "I did have a mother, you know." He set the plate aside. "You can load the dishwasher."

Too bemused to form an argument, Deanna figured out the latch on the fancy dishwasher and opened the door. Bending over, she began loading the rinsed items inside. But not even that action was familiar, since her modest apartment didn't possess even a nonfancy variety.

"Did you have regular chores as a kid, then?" Her gaze had automatically started to rise when she spoke, but it went dead still when she found her eyes nearly on a level with his rear.

One of the plates clattered as it slid into its slot too quickly and she carefully redirected her gaze from the painfully excellent cut of his custom-tailored trousers over those glutes and was grateful that he couldn't see her.

"We all had chores." His hand moved and a water glass appeared almost in front of her nose. Mindful that it probably wouldn't tolerate the same carelessness as the plate, she carefully lifted it out of his hand as he continued. "Inside the house and out," he was saying. "Until he got old enough that he realized the payment wasn't worth the chore, I used to bribe Darr into taking most of mine."

She straightened. "That sounds more like the man I know," she said wryly and caught a wisp of a smile around his lips. The first in hours.

And no matter what sort of mess she was in, she still felt as if she'd won some great prize at the sight.

"I didn't mind the yard work so much," he admitted. "It was outside at least." He looked at the window above the sink, but all that was visible were their own reflections against the darkness outside.

It was strange enough to be standing alongside him working on the dishes, much less to see their images in that windowpane.

It was far too…domestic.

Particularly when she couldn't stop thinking that, sooner or later, they were going to be sleeping in the same bedroom again.

Same bedroom.

Same bed.

She bent over the dishwasher rack again, fitting another plate into place, only this time she was careful to keep her eyes focused where they belonged. "If, uh, if you want me to, I could draft the media release for you. Maybe a few versions for you to look at." She'd done so dozens of times before for him; just not ones that dealt with such a serious, personal matter.

"Did you have to do chores?"

She straightened again. "What? Oh. Yeah." All of them, pretty much, since Gigi had usually been incapable of it. "Most kids do." She took the last dish from him and placed it in the rack, then closed the door and went out of the kitchen, back to the dining-room table where she took her time gathering up the colorful woven place mats and napkins before carrying them into the kitchen in hope that he would lose his sudden curiosity about her childhood.

He was standing where she'd left him, only he'd turned his back to the sink and his arms were crossed over his chest. His brooding gaze tracked her movements as if he were trying to calculate something while she brushed off the place mats and left them stacked on the island. She carried the cloth napkins into the laundry room next to the kitchen that she'd noticed earlier, but eventually, she couldn't pretend there was any more busywork.

He was still studying her when she stopped next to the granite-topped island again. She felt like a bug on the end of a pin, and didn't care for it at all. She lifted her hands. "What?"

"When you were a kid, what did you want to be when you grew up?"

She hadn't known what was ticking around in his mind, but she certainly hadn't expected that. He couldn't have chosen a question that would have surprised her more.

She blinked and shrugged a little. "I don't know. A ballerina for a while. Isn't that what all little girls want to be?"

"After you were older than five," he drawled.

"What did you want to be when you were five?" she returned tartly.

"A fireman, but I grew out of that. Obviously, Darr didn't." His lips twisted. "He always did have a hero complex."

She wrapped her fingers around the wrought-iron back of one of the bar stools. "You admire him." Despite his dark humor, she'd seen that already for herself.

"Not everybody has what it takes to run into a burning building when everyone else is trying to get out of it."

"I guess that's true. I've never really thought about it before," she admitted. And as nice as she considered his younger brother to have been, she was much more fascinated with what made Drew tick. It didn't seem to matter that part of her knew it wasn't wise to indulge such a fascination at all. "So after the fireman, what'd you want to be?"

"I was asking you that question, remember?"

She exhaled. "Fine. I wanted to be a pilot. You?"

"President of Fortune Forecasting."

"Even when you were a kid?" She was surprised. She'd always suspected he'd gone into the family business because it had been expected, not because it was something at which he'd turned out to be exceptionally good.

"Even then." His gaze was steady. "What stopped you from being a pilot?"

Her hands twisted around the wrought iron and the band of the engagement ring dug into her finger.

She didn't know what was spurring Drew's sudden interest, but the sooner it ended, the more comfortable she'd feel. "Money. More specifically, the lack of it. So, about that press release?"

"If you had the money now, would you still want to become one?"

"No."

"Why not?"

"Why all the questions, Drew?"

"Just trying to get to know my fiancée better."

She squelched her response just in time. For all they knew, given his father's disappearance, her position as his fiancée could well turn out to be unnecessary after all.

And in comparison to what he was going through, the reason behind her desire to be a pilot seemed utterly unimportant. She unwound her fingers from the wrought iron and rubbed her reddened palms down the sides of her jeans. "Because I realized even if I could fly off to be like my father, it still wouldn't have brought him back home to me."

His gaze stayed steady on her face and she mentally braced herself for yet another intrusion into her life.

But after a moment, all he did was unfold his arms and push away from the edge of the farmhouse-style sink. "Draft up whatever you think the release should say. I'll look at it when I get back. You can send it first thing in the morning."

Her wits felt scattered trying to keep up with him. "Where are you going?"

"Out."

He scooped a set of keys off the rack of

them by the kitchen door before quietly letting himself out into the night.

Feeling abruptly spent, Deanna could only stand there and watch him go.

Chapter 8

Deanna was talking on the phone in J.R.'s office. He'd kindly offered it for her and Drew's use after their stay in Red Rock quickly lengthened from four days to ten when she heard the slam of a door elsewhere in the house.

Drew and Jeremy must be back from town where they'd gone to see Darr at his fire station, because Isabella didn't make that much noise and J.R. was out at Lily's.

Ten days had passed since William's disappearance.

Ten torturously slow days.

And ten even more torturously...slow... nights.

She couldn't marshal her pulse that sped up just from knowing that Drew was in the house, but she could still pretend. So she focused on the task at hand—namely her telephone conversation with Fortune Forecasting's L.A.-based Human Resources director.

"Send a hard copy of the proof overnight," she finished telling Chelsea. "I'll let you know if there are any changes by the end of tomorrow, and if not, you can sign off on the brochure and get it into production." Fortune Forecasting had long been scheduled to be part of a three-day job fair in Los Angeles later that week, and the brochure was part of the printed collateral that was to be made available there. Drew had been scheduled to give a speech at the event, but she'd already arranged a replacement—a professional baseball player that Drew was friends with who was a popular figure on the motivational circuit.

She heard another door slam and a raised voice. J.R.'s. She could easily distinguish now the differences in his voice compared with Drew's and Jeremy's.

She glanced at her watch. It was the middle of the day. She still had at least a dozen calls to return on Drew's behalf, and more than twice that many emails to attend to. But the sound of

J.R.'s voice when she'd thought he was going to be gone all afternoon was unusual enough that when she hung up with Chelsea, she left the office and went to investigate.

She found them all in the great room, including Drew. Even Isabella had come out of her workroom where she had a loom on which she wove her amazing tapestries and blankets.

What surprised Deanna most, though, was the sight of Lily Fortune.

She hadn't seen the woman since the day of her nonwedding, although Deanna knew that in addition to J.R., Isabella and Jeremy had been regular visitors out to her ranch. She couldn't hazard a guess whether Drew had been. Aside from knowing that he—along with his brothers—had visited every police station, hospital and morgue in half the state, he never said where he was going when he disappeared from the hacienda every evening or what he was doing when he went.

All Deanna knew was that for the past ten days, every evening after supper—which Deanna had continued helping Isabella to prepare since that first night—he left the house and didn't return until after Deanna was in bed and asleep. Or at least pretending to be asleep.

And when morning dawned and she did wake, he'd be gone again, leaving only the impression of his head on the pillow as proof that he'd ever been there at all.

He couldn't have made it more plain that he wasn't interested in chancing any more close encounters of the intimate kind upon waking.

She looked from him to Lily, who was pacing back and forth in front of Jeremy near the windows. She was wearing jeans and a button-down plaid shirt with her hair braided down her back and couldn't have looked more different than the bride she'd been, yet she still possessed the same indefinable, elegant strength that Deanna couldn't help but admire.

"Ross has news," Isabella told Deanna quietly. "He was on the road when he called and Molly's Pride was closer than Lily's place, so he's coming here to meet with us all at once."

Deanna felt queasy. Ross was Drew's investigator cousin. And if he felt compelled to deliver his news to Lily in person...

She looked back at Drew. He'd sprawled in one of the oversize chairs that filled the space, his long, jean-clad legs crossed at the ankles. But she knew the lazy-looking position was deceptive. She could feel the tension emanating from him from across the room. Could see it in the lines bracketing his lips and the long fingers that were silently drumming against the leather arm of the chair.

Even though she'd spent plenty of time with Drew's family, she nevertheless still felt like an intruder. But she also knew that only she and Drew would know the reason why, so she made herself cross the room and perch on the ottoman that was near his chair. "Are you all right?"

His gaze slanted toward her. "Peachy."

Her lips tightened. Just sitting near him made her feel shaky inside, but that didn't mean she enjoyed his sarcasm. "I was only asking," she said under her breath.

"I know." He drummed his fingertips again. "Sorry."

She chewed the inside of her lip and managed not to close her hand over his restless one. He was wearing a brown shirt that was the same color as his eyes. She assumed he must have borrowed it from his brother because it wasn't one that had been hanging in their closet.

They'd already stayed nearly a week longer than they'd originally planned. Isabella had offered the use of their washer and dryer, which Deanna had by necessity taken up. She should have laundered Drew's things as well, but something had stopped her.

Washing his clothes, strangely enough, seemed even more personal than sleeping on opposite sides of the same bed.

She looked down at her folded hands. She'd grown accustomed to the feel of the diamond ring on her finger, but she still hadn't grown used to the sight of it there. It had been jarring from the first moment he'd slipped it on her finger. It was still jarring now.

And frightening considering the pang of… longing…that was only increasing by the day.

"Everything set for the job fair?"

She nodded, glad of the distraction, even though she was vaguely surprised that he remembered it. As large an event as it was, she'd been handling all of the arrangements for it all along. His only involvement was to have been his scheduled "motivational" rah-rah session. "Chelsea said they're expecting over five thousand people," she told him. It would be a well-orchestrated zoo.

"It's the first year you'll miss it."

She lifted her shoulder, again surprised that he'd realized that. "Chelsea and her department have things well in hand. They won't miss me." And the organizers handling the half dozen companies being represented at the fair wouldn't, either. They cared about missing Drew, but had been slightly mollified by the celebrity athlete she'd been able to produce.

"Hmm." His fingers continued drumming.

"Do you need this back?" She pulled his BlackBerry out of the pocket of her sweater and held it out. She'd been using his phone to handle all of the business calls rather than J.R. and Isabella's house line.

"Any emergencies at the office that I don't know about and need to?"

"No." Aside from the employees' anxiety caused by William's disappearance and the media's attention that had been deflected for the most part by the press release they'd issued, everything at Fortune Forecasting was at least running smoothly.

"Then, no, I don't need it." He shook his head, and because she knew she still had plenty of use for it, she slid it back into her pocket.

Her own cell phone was still turned off and shoved inside her purse. She'd listened to her mother's numerous voice mails. And she'd sent her an email that she was in Texas with her boss…on business. Not that Gigi had bought that story, which she'd told Deanna in a long voice message immediately after. Gigi didn't live under a rock, after all. She, too, had heard the news that William Fortune was missing. And she'd archly suggested that Deanna make "good use" of her time with her boss during his hour of need.

Deanna had been furious enough to return that call, but the results had been typical—Gigi accusing Deanna of abandoning her when she needed her most, and Deanna feeling guilty. So she'd told her mother to find a counselor and not to call her again until she had.

Since then, her voice mailbox had been unusually empty. Deanna still couldn't decide if that was progress or not.

A doorbell chimed and everyone jumped.

Isabella quickly hurried out of the room and just as quickly returned with Ross Fortune on her heels.

His brown gaze traveled the room, landing on Lily, who'd gone stock-still at the sight of him, holding her arms around her waist.

Everyone else rose to their feet, waiting...

"His car's been found," he said bluntly.

Jeremy moved next to Lily, as if he were afraid she might collapse. But all she did was pale. "And?" Lily's chin was lifted, but she looked braced for anything.

Ross looked only marginally better than his cousins did. His brown hair was rumpled and he had the same weary lines creasing his face. "And there's no sign of William." His voice was careful and Deanna caught the look that passed between him and the other men.

Her stomach sank and she looked toward Isabella and was grateful that the other woman had sat down again. Deanna was certain that Isabella hadn't yet confided her suspicion to her husband. And because Isabella hadn't shared with Deanna that it had been a false alarm, she assumed that her hostess's suspicion was probably even closer to certainty now.

"Where was the car?" Lily asked. She was still standing upright, but her voice had gone thin.

"Outside of Haggarty."

Deanna started at the name of the town. She remembered Darr mentioning it the day of the wedding. He'd said an accident had occurred near there.

A fatal accident.

Lily made a sound then and covered her

mouth with her hand. A moment later, she seemed to crumple.

Jeremy leaped forward, catching her in his arms before she collapsed right to the floor.

Isabella cried out, jumping out of her chair and rushing to them.

"She fainted. She needs to lie down," Jeremy said tersely. "I have smelling salts in my medical bag."

"Take her to our bedroom. It's the closest. I'll bring your bag." Isabella practically ran out of the room, leading the way for Jeremy to carry the tall woman out of the room.

Deanna watched them go. Her heart was thudding so hard she could feel it inside her head. She didn't even realize that she'd reached out for Drew's hand until she felt his fingers curl around hers in response.

"The police aren't tying that other accident together with William's." When they were gone, Ross answered the question that nobody had asked but everybody had thought. "Yet." His voice was grim as he looked from J.R. to Drew. "The other car had no signs of collision with another vehicle. They found no debris that didn't come from the car where it ran off a curve and collided with several trees before going down the embankment, so the authorities over there still maintain that it was a single-car accident. William's Mercedes, on the other hand, is at the bottom of an embankment some distance away. It's heavily shaded by trees and brush. The only reason it was found at all was because of a couple who were hiking back in there over the weekend. It's not a popular spot at all."

"I want to see the car," Drew said abruptly. J.R. nodded.

"So do I," Ross agreed. "I also want to talk to the police in Haggarty and interview the couple who found the car. And I want to do it as soon as possible while everything is fresh in their mind."

"Then let's go," Drew said immediately.

"J.R.?"

J.R. turned to see Isabella walking back into the room. "How's Lily?"

"She's coming around already. Jeremy wants her to lie down for a while, though. Her blood pressure is up and he's threatening her with a sedative if she doesn't behave." Her liquid-brown gaze flickered over Deanna and Drew, then back to her husband. "Can I talk to you for a second?"

J.R. gave a quick frown, but went to her immediately and followed her out of the room.

"Do you know how badly damaged Dad's car is?" Drew asked Ross.

His cousin shook his head. "The investigators were heading out to the site when I got the call from my contact at the Haggarty P.D., so there's no official information yet. I want to get there soon while there's still enough daylight left to see things for myself. We've already had rain since the accident, so who knows what evidence will be left to find after so many days."

J.R. returned in time to hear the tail end of Ross's comment. "You and Drew can go. I've got something else I need to take care of."

"More important than finding out where the hell Dad's gone?" Drew demanded. He gave Deanna an impatient look when she made a faint sound and squeezed his hand.

"Right now, yes," J.R. returned evenly. "I'm taking my wife into town to see her doctor."

Drew swore under his breath. "Sorry, man. Is she all right?"

"She thinks she's pregnant."

Deanna exhaled. Thank goodness.

"If she is, I'm not taking any chances with her."

Drew was nodding. "Of course." He clapped a hand on his brother's shoulder. A faint smile had mercifully replaced the drawn lines on his face. "A baby, huh? That would be some good news around here about now."

J.R. looked a little pale beneath his bemused expression, but he nodded. "That's for sure."

Ross was smiling, too. "Going to have to get used to the idea of you changing diapers," he drawled.

"Well, first, we need to make sure nothing happens this time," J.R. said. He headed out of the room again. "Call me with whatever you find, though," he added before he left.

"This time?" Ross looked at Drew, who shook his head.

"Isabella had a miscarriage several months ago," Deanna provided quietly. Because J.R. had opened the door, and Isabella herself had said that it wasn't really a secret, she didn't feel too much like she was divulging a confidence.

"How do you know that?"

Drew's incredulousness stung. Just because all she was to him was his assistant and fiancée-for-appearances'-sake didn't mean everyone else saw her that way. "I have gotten to know Isabella a little since we've been here," she reminded.

"Women talk," Ross summed up, fortunately not seeming to share Drew's surprise at all. "We'd better take separate vehicles to Haggarty. I might be there longer than you'll want to stay. It's rough terrain. Make sure you take one of the four-wheel drives." His gaze ran over Deanna. "And wear boots if you've got 'em."

She started, watching the man leave the room. He assumed she'd be accompanying them.

Drew's brooding gaze trapped hers. "Do you want to go?" He sounded doubtful.

It would be a simple matter to tell him that she didn't. She had enough Fortune Forecasting matters to take care of for him to easily fill the rest of the afternoon.

But she didn't for the simple reason that—no matter what they found or didn't find—she wanted to be there for him.

And that desire had nothing to do with being a good assistant.

She lifted her chin. "Do you want me to go?"

His eyes narrowed. "What are you mad about?"

"I'm not mad." Irritated, maybe, that he so easily thought of her only as his assistant. Which was an irritation in itself—but with herself—for being foolish enough to think otherwise. "Yes or no? Your cousin is waiting."

His lips thinned. "Yes," he snapped.

"All right, then," she snapped back.

"Go find some boots."

"I have tennis shoes and I have the high heels I brought to go with that dress for the wedding." She wiggled her feet. "These will have to do because I am not raiding Isabella's closet."

"Why not?"

"Because she hasn't offered and it wouldn't feel right," she hissed under her breath. "So are we going to go or not?"

He gave her a strange look, as if she'd grown a third eye, but nodded. "We're going."

Deanna could say she wasn't mad about something, but everything Drew knew about women told him otherwise as she sat beside him in the truck they'd borrowed from Molly's Pride.

Aside from the telephone calls that Deanna fielded while they followed Ross's truck out of town, and the messages that she tapped out on Drew's BlackBerry, she didn't say more than a half dozen words directly to him.

If that wasn't a woman pissed off about something, what was it?

And as they drove, Drew found it easier to puzzle over the workings of his assistant's mind than it was to think about what they might find once they reached their destination.

"No, Maggie, you'll have to tell Horning that Drew's unavailable for an interview right now." She was on the phone again, this time with one of the secretaries. "He knows exactly why Drew's out of town, which is why he's calling. And I know what he can be like, but don't let him bully you. Yes, I know I could call him for you, but you can handle it. Just apologize for the inconvenience, but be firm. We'll reschedule an interview when we can. Don't worry. You'll be fine. Yes. Call me back if you need me."

Drew glanced at her when she hung up. "John Horning is a pain in the neck." And right now, he had even less desire to talk to the man than usual.

"I know that and you know that. But he's also one of the most popular investigative reporters in San Diego. He's not going to be that easy to avoid if he's intent on getting a statement from you beyond the press release we issued. He's obviously following the story—

he'll learn soon enough that your dad's car has been found." His BlackBerry rang again and she answered it.

Her gaze slid toward him a moment later. She pressed a button, then held the phone toward him. "It's on mute. You can handle this call yourself. It's Stephanie Hughes."

He waved off the phone. "Get rid of her."

Deanna made a face. She pressed a button and put the phone back to her ear. "I'm sorry, Ms. Hughes. Unfortunately, Drew is unavailable right now. Can I give him a message?" She suddenly winced and held the phone out from her ear.

Drew could hear the strident, feminine tones spewing out of the phone, every third word an expletive and every fourth, Deanna's name.

He exhaled roughly and grabbed the phone out of her hand. "Steph? It's Drew. I told you things were over a month ago. It had nothing to do with Deanna then, but considering the way you're talking about her, it does now." He hung up while the woman was still swearing at him, and tossed the phone onto the console. "Sorry about that. She heard about the engagement from a clerk at Zondervan's." Where she'd probably gone to find out the value of the bracelet Deanna had procured as an exit gift from Drew. In the month that Drew had seen Stephanie, he'd been hard-pressed to decide if she was more interested in his connections or his money. Either way, he'd gotten tired of the woman even more quickly than usual.

"I gathered that." Denim rustled as Deanna crossed her jean-clad legs and looked out the window beside her.

Ross was slowing ahead of him, and Drew did the same.

"Has she been calling a lot?"

The ends of Deanna's hair slid over her shoulder. "Only this once. You've had calls from Erin, Sonya, Mindy and Alexa, though. Several, each, actually. Oh, and Belinda, too." She gave him a bland look. "She left you quite an…inventive…message on your voice mail. I saved it for you."

He actually felt his neck get hot. "I met her a few weeks ago. She's a model."

"A lingerie model." She'd looked back out the window, sounding bored. "Yes. I heard that part, too. Unintentionally."

He could only imagine what else she might have heard. Belinda Reeves was nothing if not verbal about what she wanted. Namely, him, in some definitely adventurous ways, which she'd made more than plain when he'd met her at a friend's beach house. "I haven't slept with her." He hadn't ruled it out, but realized now that the possibility had lost its appeal.

Primarily because he couldn't get his assistant out of his head.

Deanna didn't even budge. "That's none of my business."

"If not yours, then whose? You're my fiancée."

At that, her head did turn. Her hazel eyes were cool. "So you do remember."

"Do you think it's something I'm likely to forget?" His hand tightened around the steering wheel. Every freaking time he walked into the bedroom they were sharing, it was the only thing he could think about.

She wore his ring. They were sleeping— more or less—in the same bed.

It was making him insane.

She was the only woman on the planet he'd ever wanted and not done something about it.

Which was why he'd been spending as little time around her as was humanly possible.

"Look," he began carefully, "I know this hasn't been easy on you. I've dumped everything from back at the office on you and—"

"I don't care about that."

"And you've obviously had to field more

personal calls than I expected. I'm sorry about that, too."

"It's nothing I don't deal with in San Diego."

His patience was thinning and he exhaled roughly. "Then what's the burr you've got under your blanket all about?"

"Nothing that I'm not smart enough to get over," she said coolly.

Which was no answer at all.

He tried another tack. "Have you talked to your mother?"

She gave him a suspicious look. "Not in the past few days. Why?"

He shrugged. Given the temper on her face, he figured now wouldn't be the best time to admit that he'd called Gigi Gurney himself several days earlier. She'd been positively simpering when she'd realized who he was, and had girlishly giggled and promised that, of course, she was willing to go to counseling if that would make her little Deedee happy. He'd felt in need of a strong bolt of coffee afterward just to get the woman's overblown, cloying sweetness out of his head.

Deanna really was nothing at all like her mother.

Thank God.

He realized Ross was slowing to a crawl,

pulling off the side of the empty road onto a very narrow shoulder, and Drew pulled in behind him to park. "Wait here."

He waited until Deanna nodded, her expression as abruptly solemn as he felt inside, and got out of the truck.

He met Ross halfway. "Is this the spot?"

Ross shook his head. He unfolded a map and spread it out against the side of his truck. "From what the boys in Haggarty told me, William's car probably went off about a mile up." He stabbed a sharply curving line on the map. "They warned me that there's no spot to stop there, though."

Drew didn't know if he was relieved or not that he wasn't standing in the exact spot his father's vehicle had left the highway. He looked from the map to the road ahead and realized then that leading from the shoulder ahead of Ross's truck was a road of sorts.

Dirt and steep as hell, the glorified path cut through the tall brush from the main road and disappeared into the trees. "That how we get down there?"

His cousin nodded. "The road goes about two miles before it dead-ends at a dry creek. We'll have to go on foot the rest of the way." He folded the map until only one square section showed. He traced his finger in a circle around a small area. "That'll give you an idea of the lay." He handed the map to Drew. "How long's it been since you've gone four-wheeling?"

Drew grimaced. "Not long, but that was for entertainment."

Ross grunted. "Sure you're up to this? It's not going to be a picnic to see."

"Yeah."

"What about Deanna?"

Drew looked over his shoulder at the truck. Despite the distance, he could see the little frown lines on her forehead. Could see the worry in her wide eyes. "She'll be all right."

"Yeah, well, she looks like she's about ready to vomit."

Drew frowned. Deanna did look almost as sick as he felt. "She wouldn't have come with me if she didn't want to be here."

"You sure?"

He nodded.

There were more than a few things he was realizing he hadn't known about Deanna Gurney.

She jogged every morning for an hour before she showered with that green apple–

scented shampoo of hers and headed into the hacienda's kitchen for a cup of hot tea.

Tea. Not coffee. Turns out she didn't even drink the stuff.

He'd always appreciated her incredibly bright mind and used it to his advantage. But now he knew she had a body that was made to be worshipped to go along it. And he knew that her mossy-green eyes turned to emerald when her emotions were high, which was far more often than he would ever have suspected of his pragmatic, all-about-business assistant.

He'd learned all of that in the ten days that had passed since he'd woken up in bed with her, her seductive body unintentionally all but glued to his.

And there were an infinite number of things more to learn that taunted him.

Tempted him.

But the one thing he did know about Deanna?

"I'm sure. She's stronger than you think," he told Ross.

Then he pushed the map in his pocket and walked back to the truck.

Chapter 9

"Oh my God." Deanna's hushed voice seemed to echo around the small clearing where William Fortune's luxury sedan had finally come to a crashing stop.

Luxury was no more.

The hood of the car was caved in thanks to the gigantic boulder, which was undoubtedly what had stopped the car from heading even farther along the wooded ravine where they'd found it. All but one of the windows were shattered out, and the roof of the car was dented in as if it had rolled.

Probably more than once.

And who knew what was responsible for

the mangled rear of the car and the passenger door that hung off its frame in a gaping tilt as if it, too, wanted to scream.

She turned her eyes away from the sight.

"You okay?" Drew was standing next to her. Unlike her, he didn't seem out of breath at all. Not from the strenuous walk they'd had once they'd left the trucks behind, nor from the grim sight of his father's demolished vehicle.

"I should be asking you that." She pulled in a deep breath, scented strongly of scrub brush and dirt and biting cold air. She hadn't realized how tiring it would be to walk on the shifting gravel and rock of a not entirely dry creek bed. But that had been easier than try-ing to navigate the unfriendly land beside it.

Her jeans were caked with mud up to her knees. It even squished between her toes where it had worked into her shoes and through her socks. And neither Drew nor Ross looked any better.

"I'd rather see it than not know," Drew told her. Like her, he was carrying one of the bot-tles of water that Ross had come prepared with and he handed it to her. "Finish it if you need more," he offered.

She took the bottle, though she had no in-tention of drinking his share in addition to her own, and watched him work his way over and around the tumble of rocks and boulders where his father's car was lodged.

Ross was already crawling around in the front seat of it. Or as much of the front seat as was left.

She didn't know how either one of them could bear it and even though she was glad to have accompanied Drew, glad in some deep part of her that he'd wanted her with him, she finally had to simply look away from the wreckage.

She propped the two water bottles on the sandy, graveled ground next to a weathered, rotting log, and carefully picked her way around the area, seeing nothing but more mud.

More rocks.

More scraping, poking shrubs and scarred trees.

How could William have walked away from that devastatingly mangled vehicle, much less through such inhospitable terrain?

"Watch out." Ross spoke beside her and she stopped cold, startled nearly out of her wits. He pointed. "That's a footprint." His heavy boots—much more suited to hiking than her tennis shoes—circled a small area.

All she saw was a drying patch of mud.

He pulled out a slender digital camera and crouched down, taking several shots of the patch at differing angles. Then he rose, and slowly followed some path that Deanna couldn't detect, stopping every now and then to crouch down again and take more pictures. Before long, he'd disappeared into a tangle of bushes that were so tall that she could barely see the top of his head.

She looked back at the car, and even knowing what to expect, still felt the sight of it in some deep, uneasy portion of her stomach.

Drew was still inside the front of the car, his wide shoulders wedged into the driver's seat now. His legs were braced outside of the car against the pitched ground.

She blew out a long breath, hoped she wouldn't be sick and moved over to the side of the car.

Inside, she could see the limp remains of spent safety airbags. Dirt and stones littered the seats and the floor where it had come in through the windows. The windshield was a mass of spidery cracks.

"There really is no blood," Drew murmured. "Not even the smallest spatter."

Deanna focused on his face instead of the wreckage. Ross had told them that the police who'd investigated the scene had reported that there wasn't any evidence of human injury, but it still seemed hard to believe. "I don't know how anyone can even tell, considering how much debris and dirt there is." There was even a small tree branch caught in the seat beside him.

Drew looked at her. "I rolled a car when I was a senior in college." He grimaced and looked away. His hand brushed over the passenger seat. Dust puffed up and glimmered in the fractured sunlight slanting through the windshield. "Three of us were in the car. We all ended up with plenty of cuts and bruises and that was nothing as bad as this. But there was still blood smeared on a few windows and the seats and doors."

Deanna hastily shut off the images that brought to her mind. "Were you hurt badly?"

"That's where I got this." He touched the small scar near his hairline. "But none of us were really hurt. Thank God."

"How'd it happen?"

"Being stupid. As usual." He grimaced. "We'd driven down to Rocky Point in Mexico to party and were on our way back to the States. I swerved to avoid a guy pushing a cart who came out of nowhere. Missed him.

Rolled the car. The only good thing was that I wasn't drinking or it would have been a helluva mess."

He let out a breath and shook his head again. "The search dogs the police brought through here would have scented Dad's blood if there'd been any to find. Inside or outside the car."

"Then maybe the airbags did what they were supposed to do," Deanna posed.

"Maybe." He leaned over and swept his hand inside the glove compartment where the door was already hanging askew. "It's empty."

"The police could have emptied it."

"Hmm." He sat back up again. His hands circled the steering wheel that was sitting at an unnaturally close angle to the seat and his body. "I wonder if Dad was even in the car when it went down the embankment."

"Like he'd gotten thrown from the car before it went over?" She looked upward, trying to follow the line the car seemed to have taken. But they were too deep in the ravine to see the road.

"Maybe."

"Or do you still think there's a possibility of foul play?"

"Ross doesn't. If it were a kidnapping, we'd have gotten a ransom demand by now."

"What do you think?"

"I don't know what to think." He opened the console. Pulled out a small notepad and flipped through the pages. Deanna could see that they were blank. "Not anymore." He tossed the notepad back in the console and closed it with a snap. Then he reached up and flipped down the sun visor.

A slip of paper fell from it and hit his knee, then slid onto the floor.

He reached down, his hands sweeping for it.

"I've got it." She could see where the white square had fallen, almost beneath the seat and she knelt next to him, reaching around his legs. Her muddy shoe slipped a few inches just as she felt the slick paper under her fingertip and she steadied herself with the closest object.

His thigh.

She hastily adjusted her footing and let go of him before grabbing the item as she straightened again.

"Here." She handed him what turned out to be a black-and-white photograph of a dark-haired woman.

"That's my mother." His thumb slowly flicked the corner of the photograph as he stared thoughtfully through the crackled windshield.

"And the baby she's holding?"

He didn't even glance at the picture again. "J.R."

Deanna's teeth worried the inside of her cheek when he said nothing more. But a moment later, she heard rustling and looked over to see Ross emerging from the bushes again.

"Seen enough?" he asked as he walked closer.

She had. More than enough. But this wasn't about her and she knew that if Drew wanted to stay, then she would suck up her horror and stay with him for as long as he needed to be there.

But he was working himself out of the crushed-in car and she moved away to give him more space to maneuver.

When he was out, he looked at his cousin. "Find anything useful?"

"A boatload of partial footprints." Which didn't seem to make Ross very happy, judging by the frown on his face. "Most of them probably made by the police when they came through with the tracking dogs. Hard to tell, particularly after the rain. From what I could see, the shoe treads all looked pretty rugged, like hiking boots. Because we don't know what William was wearing—" He broke off, grimacing, and slid his small camera back in his jacket pocket. "It's going to take us a while to get back to the trucks and we'll lose the light if we don't get started soon."

"I've seen enough of the car." Drew closed his hand over Deanna's shoulder and nudged her forward.

"Wait." She turned back after several steps to grab their water bottles and hurried back to them and then, aside from the slip of gravel under their feet, they silently began their trek back to their trucks.

Just as Ross had predicted, by the time they reached the two vehicles, the sun was hanging low, reddening the sky with an impossibly beautiful sunset.

Ross pulled two fresh water bottles out of the pack in his vehicle and held them out. "I'm going to book it to Haggarty. I can still catch the guy who caught the call before his shift ends. You coming or heading back?"

Drew tossed their empty bottles into the truck bed and took the fresh supply, handing one to Deanna. "Back."

"I'll let you know if I learn anything. Drive careful up the road." And then with a wave, he climbed in his big truck and was heading off, bumping over the rocky bank of the creek bed.

Deanna headed around their truck for the passenger side, but stopped short of getting in when she realized Drew hadn't moved.

Instead, he'd balanced his water bottle on the side of the truck and remained there with his arms propped next to the water.

He was holding up the photograph.

"He used to keep this same picture on his desk at the office. A larger one, I mean." He squared the picture between his long fingers. "He had six in all. One of the two of them on their wedding day. And one each of her with all of us as babies."

"That's lovely," she said softly.

"Why'd he keep this picture in his car?"

"What do you mean?"

"Why not one of Lily?"

"Sentiment," Deanna suggested. "You just said how he kept the ones in his office."

"True," he mused softly and looked at the photo again. Then he smiled slightly. "I remember one time she was redecorating Dad's office for him and took away all those old pictures. Gave him one framed picture instead— some family portrait she'd made us all get spit-shined for when I was in junior high. But he made her bring all the other ones back."

He glanced across the truck bed at Deanna, holding up the photo between his fingers. "She wanted to know why he wanted those old photos when there was such a nice new one where she was looking the best she'd ever looked in her life, and he told her because the others were reminders of every moment in his life when his love for her had doubled."

Her heart squeezed. Not just from the story, but because Drew was actually sharing it. She almost didn't want to say a word, afraid he'd stop if she did. But she couldn't keep silent. She set her water bottle inside on her seat. "He must have loved her very much."

"We all did," he murmured. He looked back at the photograph. "She would have liked you."

She swallowed. "Why?"

"You're here. Even after I tried to get you to go, you're here."

Just that easily, she felt tears burning deep behind her eyes.

She blinked them back, hard, before he could notice and moved around the truck beside him.

She slipped the photograph out of his fingers and looked into the long-ago face of his mother. Molly Fortune was sitting up in a hospital bed wearing a pale-colored bed jacket and staring into the camera with a serene smile.

It was a small photograph. Maybe three inches square. But the woman's contented happiness as she held her firstborn son in her arms still managed to shine out of it.

Deanna couldn't recall ever seeing photos of her mother holding her as a baby. If there had been photos from her childhood, they'd disappeared somewhere along the way.

"Your mother probably kept a baby book for each of you," she guessed. Along with the woman he described, the image in the photograph seemed to suggest that Molly had been the kind of mother who would have done so. As well as making sure they had family portraits through the years.

Something else that had been absent from Deanna's upbringing. A happy-looking family, recorded for posterity.

For the Gurneys, there had been no happiness. No family. Just a mother who basically blamed her only daughter for existing.

Deanna focused on Drew, who was looking at her with a small frown.

"Didn't your mom keep a baby book?"

"I doubt it." She shrugged, not entirely comfortable having the focus back on her. "If she did, she's never showed it to me. And Gigi's not big on that sort of thing anyway."

"What is she big on, aside from the home shopping channels?"

"Grandiose dreams of finding the perfect romance."

"Sounds like a lot of women I know."

Deanna made a face. "She just chooses to continually look in the wrong place."

"Is there a right place?"

"Don't ask me. I'm not the one with the experience. Where'd you meet your ex-wife?"

"College. But that doesn't count because it obviously wasn't real."

"Or she wouldn't have cheated on you?"

His lips twisted. "Presumably."

She chewed the inside of her lip. "Cheating has no place in true love."

"So you've been in love? With who? That Mike guy?"

"Mark." She shook her head. "And no. But you still haven't said whether or not you had a baby book."

He gave her a sideways look that told her he knew she was being evasive, then shrugged. "Yeah. Baby books for all of us. Scrapbooks. My mother did 'em all. Filled with hair from our first haircuts and birthday cards and report cards once we got into school." He grinned crookedly. "Even though some of those report cards definitely weren't worth saving, at least on my part."

"I find that hard to believe."

"Why?"

She laughed a little. "Because you're fiercely brilliant, which you very well know. Aside from the whole spelling thing, that is."

"Well, believe it. I goofed off more in school than I should have. Used to drive my father crazy."

"And your mother?"

Drew's wry smile died. "She'd shake her head and tell me that she knew I could do better." He was silent for a moment, remembering.

So he had done better. Or at least he'd tried to.

His throat suddenly felt tight. "She gave all the books to each of us when she got sick."

Deanna's hand squeezed his shoulder. "She looks like a beautiful woman," she said softly and handed him the photograph. "Inside and out."

He took the photograph, too aware of the way his fingers brushed hers.

His memories of his mother were so clear they were just as much a physical ache inside him as the other unassuaged ache he'd developed for Deanna.

But remembering his mother was easier than thinking about that mangled car. And wondering what on God's earth had become of his father.

Was the picture that William had kept in his car significant? Or was it, like Deanna suggested, simply sentiment?

He turned his back against the side of the truck and his arm brushed against the soft fullness of her breast.

He squinted into the sunset, very aware of the fact that Deanna didn't take a step back. Didn't put a breathing space carefully between them as she usually did.

She remained right where she was, facing him, one arm propped against the side of the truck bed.

Or maybe it was just easier talking about things he usually didn't because Deanna was watching him and her eyes were soft in the rosy light. Almost as soft as the feel of her body when he brushed against her.

"She was beautiful," he said abruptly. "I grew up hearing my father tell her that, and she'd always blush and wave away his words and tell him she was never going to be winning any beauty contests. But we all knew that wasn't what he meant."

Deanna tilted her head slightly. Her cheek rested on her hand. "You were lucky."

He'd known that, but never more dearly until he'd realized they were losing her. "She never let anyone down." The laugh that hit him came out of nowhere. "Not that she was a saint. Man, did she have a temper. And she wouldn't let anything slip by her."

"Ah." Deanna gave him a knowing look. "I suppose you tried, though."

He smiled. "Hell, yeah. And not just me. We all did. Except for maybe J.R. He was always a pretty straight arrow." He gave a short chuckle. "One time when I was fourteen, a friend of mine and I swiped his dad's car keys—it was a classic Mustang he'd restored—and we went joyriding. Tommy sideswiped a Dumpster outside a bar and ran into a brick fence. We weren't hurt, but the police hauled us down to the station and put us in a cell. Scared the holy hell out of us. Told us we were going to be there overnight. Maybe a lot of overnights."

"Good grief. You were only fourteen?" Deanna looked shocked. He wasn't sure if it was because of the stunt they'd pulled or the jail issue.

"Nearly fifteen. Figuring we were going to be driving soon enough." They'd been cocky little idiots. "So once we're in jail, we make our one phone call we're allowed. Shaking in our boots, scared out of our minds. Tommy calls his folks, who are pretty damn furious about the car, but tell him they're on their way. Then I call my father, figuring he'll use his influence to get us off the hook altogether, 'cause there was no way that one of the sons of William Fortune was going to be run in for some mostly harmless fun. But he said no way. That we deserved to spend the night in jail. Said it would be a good lesson."

"Ouch." She winced. "What'd you do?"

He shrugged. "Tommy's folks came down as promised and he was released to them, but I had to go back to the cell."

"For how long?"

At the time, it had felt like an eternity. "Most of the night. But about three o'clock in the morning, one of the officers came and got me. My mom had come to bail me out after all." He shook his head, remembering. "She was seriously pissed. Didn't want to hear any excuses. Told me to shut up and get in the car.

But the worst of it was that I knew I'd disappointed her."

"So what happened?"

"Right before we got home, she told me that just because she loved me didn't mean she always had to like me. But no matter what, she would always be there." And she had been, until cancer had stolen her right out from under their noses.

His jaw tightened. According to William, Drew's footloose, bachelor lifestyle would have disappointed Molly, too.

Deanna shifted and took the photograph again. "Always being there. That seems the mark of true beauty to me," she murmured. Then she slid the small picture inside the lapel pocket of the shirt he'd borrowed from J.R., and softly patted it.

Her gaze lifted to his, a faint smile on her lips.

Always being there.

Just like Deanna.

Her palm started to move away from his chest and he caught her hand, holding it in place. "Yeah." His voice was suddenly coming from somewhere deep and gruff. "That's beauty."

The curve on her lips slowly died.

Her eyes widened for a breath of a second, giving him a glimpse into something even softer, even more inviting, than the inadvertent brush of her body, before she suddenly blinked.

He felt her hand start to slide out from beneath his.

"Don't."

She went still.

Her hair looked even more deeply red in the setting sunlight and he lifted his other hand, threading his fingers through the strands, slowly sliding it away from her sun-kissed cheek.

"Drew—"

He pressed his thumb across her lips, silencing whatever it was she was going to say.

If it was a protest, he didn't want to fight it.

If it was some logical argument, he didn't want to debate it.

And if it was a challenge?

At that moment, he was beyond trying to win it.

Instead, he skimmed his fingertips along the line of her jaw and wondered if she knew just how fine her skin felt, or how delicate her bones felt. Or how intensely fascinating he found it watching the long, lovely line of her throat work when she swallowed—nervously?—or how much he wanted to touch his tongue to the base of her throat, right where he figured her pulse was beating...

He watched her eyelids flicker, then go heavy when his fingertips found the nape of her neck beneath that wealth of thick, silky hair.

Her chin slowly lifted. But those eyes didn't close. Instead, her emerald gaze searched his.

What did she see?

Her boss? The man she claimed to believe was a good man? Or maybe the fallible guy who was not only a disappointment to the man he'd admired most in the world, but to the mother he still couldn't believe was gone?

And maybe it was none of them.

Maybe right then he was just a man.

A man who wanted her even when he tried not to.

The fingers he was still holding captured against his chest curled. She leaned closer into him. "Don't look at me like that if you're not going to kiss me," she whispered.

So he did.

He slowly brushed his lips over hers. Explored the shape of her full lower lip, tasted the faint bow of her upper and absorbed the soft, soft, feel of the faint sigh she gave.

It might as well have been the first kiss he'd ever had for the way it shook him.

And when he finally stopped to pull in a breath and pressed his forehead against hers, still holding her close, he realized it could have been the last kiss he'd ever need for the way it soothed him.

Her free arm came up, wrapping behind him, her hand cradling his head.

He felt her tremble.

Or maybe it was him who was shaking.

Either way, it scared the hell out of him in a way that a jail cell never had when he'd been a stupid, foolish kid.

He lifted his head.

The sun was even lower. The sunset dwindling.

"We should get back."

Deanna had tears in her eyes as she looked up at him and the sight of them had something that had nothing whatsoever to do with sex or grief aching inside him.

She nodded. Moistened her lips and looked down as she stepped away from him. Then she picked up his water bottle that had fallen to the ground without his notice and handed it to him before silently walking around the truck and climbing inside and quietly shutting the door.

He took one last look along the creek bed that had led to his father's car. But he had no more answers when it came to his missing father than he did when it came to the woman sitting in the truck waiting for him.

So he did the only thing he could do.

He climbed in behind the wheel beside her, and they drove away.

Chapter 10

They made the trip back to Molly's Pride in silence.

It was dark out when Drew stopped in front of the house to drop her off and Deanna climbed out. Her legs felt stiff, not just from the unaccustomed trek they'd made, but also because the mud on her jeans had dried and turned hard.

"I'm going to take a shower," she told him.

"Is that a warning?"

Had she meant it as one? Or had she meant it as an invitation?

She didn't know. Particularly after everything that had happened that afternoon. After the way he'd talked.

After he'd kissed her the way he had and destroyed once and for all the notion that she had any semblance of control where her feelings for him were concerned.

She looked at him. In the interior light of the truck, his hooded gaze was steady, but gave no hint whatsoever of his thoughts. If he'd been as moved by that kiss as she'd been. Or if he was afraid she'd make something out of it that she shouldn't.

Maybe all it had meant to him was a moment of...comfort...in a difficult period.

Her fingers curled around the door handle. "Do you need it to be a warning?"

"Probably."

Her heart clutched.

And even though she was no closer to understanding what emotions were going on behind those inscrutable brown eyes, she made herself nod. "Then that's what it is," she said before closing the truck door.

Then she backed away as he put the truck in motion and drove toward the set of outbuildings next to the barn.

"So how bad was it?"

Startled, she whirled around to see Isabella

standing inside the opened doorway of the house, light shining out around her like some sort of halo.

The other woman meant the accident site, of course, not the effect that Drew Fortune was having on her heart.

"Devastating," Deanna answered. Which answered both.

She brushed her hands down the sides of her filthy jeans and headed toward the door. "The car was a mess, but there was no sign of William at all. Drew wonders if he was even in the car."

Isabella was nodding. "Ross called J.R. and filled him in. I think that's something they're all wondering."

"And Lily? How's she doing?"

"Her faith is unswerving, that's how she's doing. More than once she said how strongly she feels that Ryan is watching out for William." Isabella drew in a long breath. "Whether or not that's good, she was still steady enough to want to go home after we heard from Ross. Jeremy went with her. He's going to stay with her for a while and make sure she has no more episodes like she did here. Evidently, he arranged for a leave of absence so he could stay on in Red Rock until things are more…settled."

"That's good."

"I think so." Her gaze traveled over Deanna. "By the looks of you, it must not have been a walk in the park getting there."

"It wasn't. I'm aiming straight for the shower. But I shouldn't even walk through your house."

Isabella just waved away the words as she backed into the house and closed the door after Deanna. "You can borrow some clothes. You're taller than I am, but I'm sure I have a few things that would work."

"I don't want to impose any more than I already have."

"Oh, now that's just silly." Isabella tucked her arm through Deanna's as they headed along the hallway. "If I'd been thinking straight at all, I would have thought to offer before. You must think I'm a terrible hostess."

"I think you've had plenty on your mind," Deanna assured, "and none of us expected for us to be here this long. But—" she looked down at herself again, thinking about the meager contents of their guest closet that she'd laundered more than once already "—maybe a pair of pants would be handy while I get these jeans washed. Assuming they'll even come clean."

Isabella smiled. "They will. You're no muddier than J.R. has been on occasion." They'd reached Deanna and Drew's guest room door. "I'll bring several things in for you, not just one pair of pants. And if there's something you need that I don't think of, just say so. Please."

"Thanks." Her practical nature overrode her natural inclination not to impose any more than she already felt she was doing. "So, how did the doctor visit go?"

"Wonderfully." Isabella's smile told the story, though, and Deanna was struck by the similarity between her hostess's expression and the one that Molly Fortune had been wearing in the photograph.

She gave the other woman a hug, her true delight almost enough to drown out the tinge of envy she felt. "Congratulations. I'm so happy for you all."

"Thank you." Isabella returned the hug. "And thank you. For listening that day. You're very easy to talk to, you know. You have a very sympathetic ear." Then she stepped away and smiled again. "I'll get those clothes while you clean up. J.R. insists we plan a little celebration later this week, even if the timing is bad."

"I don't think there is bad timing when it comes to celebrating a new baby."

"Which makes you sound like J.R.," Isabella pointed out, looking amused as she turned toward her own room.

Deanna closed herself in the bedroom and went straight through to the bathroom. She flipped on the shower and peeled out of her clothes. Her jeans were so stiff they practically stood up on their own.

She started to step into the shower, but went stock-still when she heard movement in the bedroom.

"Just me," Isabella called out. "I put some things on the bed." And then Deanna heard the door close again.

Her shoulders slumped. What had she expected? That Drew would have changed his mind?

She sighed and stepped into the shower. And although it was easy enough to wash away the grime from the day, it wasn't at all easy to wash away the wish that he would have.

And impossible altogether to wash away the realization that she was irrevocably, wholeheartedly in love with her boss.

* * *

Drew sat on the bed in the bedroom, listening to the sound of the shower running.

He didn't have to work hard summoning an image in his head of Deanna standing beneath the spray, water flowing over her limbs, turning her hair to wet fire and her skin to wet silk.

He shoved his hands through his hair. Pressed the heel of his palm against his closed eyes.

The images remained.

And it was only when he realized his fist was making a crumpled mess of the stack of clothes that were sitting on the bed beside him, did he realize, too, that the water had stopped running.

He made an attempt at smoothing the stack of clothes.

He had been deliberately spending as little time as possible in this room they shared. He'd walked nearly every inch of Molly's Pride. He'd sat in the bar at Red until closing time. He'd sat on the freaking back porch until the sun was nearly ready to dawn in the sky.

But could he make himself move off the foot of the bed just then, even knowing what sort of danger he was inviting?

His nerves tightened as he heard the creak

of the bathroom door. He stared down at his mud-caked boots, way too aware of the mirror across from him that would have reflected her in the doorway, if he'd allowed himself to look. "You're not alone," he announced abruptly.

"I see that," she answered after a moment.

He heard her soft footsteps on the floor and in his periphery, knew that she'd stopped at the closet door, because he could see her bare feet.

And her bare calves.

Hell.

His gaze lifted to the mirror, just long enough for him to know that she had a bath towel wrapped around her torso.

Sweat broke out on his brow and started creeping down his spine. He'd never thought of terry cloth as an instrument of seduction, until the day she'd lost hers right in front of his very eyes.

"You done in there?" His voice was rough.

"Yes." She plucked one of the garments off the stack sitting beside him and shook it out. It was a yellow dress that looked just like Isabella, and nothing like Deanna's usual severe style.

And he was damned if he didn't want to see it on her.

And off.

"Good." He shoved off the bed and brushed past her, heading into the bathroom himself.

It was filled with steam, but that would be solved quickly enough, because the only thing he needed on himself right now—because having her wasn't an option—was cold water.

And a lot of it.

He shut the door between them and nearly swallowed a groan as the smell of her seemed to hang in the steamy air. The clothes that she'd discarded were lying in a heap in one corner. The jeans were as filthy as his own and the minuscule strip of filmy white that was resting on top looked even whiter as a result.

A vibration in his jeans pocket startled the hell out of him, and he muttered an oath, looking away from Deanna's skimpy panties.

He'd forgotten he'd shoved his phone in his pocket after he'd returned J.R.'s truck to the oversize garage where the ranch vehicles were kept, and he pulled it out now, looking at the display. Stephanie Hughes.

He grimaced and silenced the vibration.

Even if he hadn't already ended things with the woman, the minimal interest he'd had in her would have been blown out of the water by the tidal wave that had become Deanna.

He pushed the phone back in his pocket and opened the bathroom door, leaning out, and knew he was a dog when disappointment snagged at him that Deanna had already pulled on the bright yellow dress and was standing in front of the mirror, working a comb through her wet hair.

Not because the dress didn't look nice. It did, particularly against her satiny-smooth, tanned skin.

But because he knew only too well that she looked even better with nothing on at all.

She was giving him a startled look through the mirror's reflection. "What?"

He barely managed to unscramble his thoughts. "Remember I mentioned Red? The restaurant?" He didn't wait for her wary nod. "We'll go there for dinner," he said abruptly.

She lowered her comb, still watching him through the mirror. "Why?"

"Because after this afternoon, we need a break from everything." God knows he did.

Of course, the logical thing would have been to take a break from the other source of his problems—her—too.

But he'd been trying to do that every night when she headed off to bed, and it had been failing him miserably.

"And I figure I owe you something. You know." He felt strangely inept and didn't particularly like it. "For handling everything at the office for me the way you have been. You've been taking care of everything for me and…and I owe you."

She looked over her shoulder directly at him then. Her brows pulled together. "I've been trying to do my job."

"And you've basically been doing mine, as well," he returned. "You've managed to keep everyone on task in San Diego and Los Angeles."

"Because everyone in both offices knows how to do their jobs," she pointed out.

"Maybe," he allowed. "But I just want you to know that everything you've done hasn't gone unnoticed."

Her eyes narrowed slightly. "Put it in my next performance review."

"Dammit, Deanna, I'm trying to show some appreciation here."

Her eyebrows shot up. "Fine," she said mildly. "We'll go out to dinner, then."

"Good." He pushed the door shut between them and shook his head. Why had he ever thought she was the least complicated, most predictable woman he'd ever met?

His gaze landed on the filmy white panties again.

The only thing predictable about her was turning out to be his increasingly unquenchable interest in everything about her.

He muttered a low oath again, directed solely at himself, and flipped on the shower.

Cold.

"You're right." Two hours later, Deanna sat back in her chair and folded her napkin, setting it beside her dinner plate. "The food here is wonderful."

Sitting across the small round table from her, Drew smiled faintly. "There's a reason why Red's made a name for itself well beyond Red Rock. The food can't be beat."

Even as often as she warned herself otherwise, Deanna knew that ninety percent of the appeal that evening for her was Drew himself.

He'd set himself out to be charming, keeping her amused with no seeming effort at all, and not once dwelling on either his father, or the company that he was willing to marry her to get.

For a seeming gesture of appreciation for her work of late, if she hadn't known better, the evening would have had all the trappings of romance.

But her head did know better, even if the rest of her kept getting caught up in him.

Obviously, the appeal for the rest of the diners was the restaurant itself, which was housed in a converted hacienda that Drew told her dated back to Texas's early statehood.

Even on a weeknight at the relatively late hour, the main dining room—which struck Deanna as blatantly romantic with its seductive dark woods and touches of passionate color—was still packed. Marcos Mendoza, Isabella's handsome half brother who managed the restaurant, was frequently on the floor, visiting with his patrons, his flashing white smile clearly as much an attraction to the female part of the crowd as was the excellent fare. He'd met Drew and Deanna at the door when they'd arrived and even as consuming as her emotions for Drew were, she was no exception to that. Isabella was a beautiful woman and her half brother was an equally arresting man and he seemed quite at home helming the busy restaurant.

"We can't leave without having Maria's famous flan, though," Drew was saying as he poured the last measure of sangria into their glasses.

"I couldn't possibly eat another bite," Deanna protested. She hadn't even been able to finish her entrée, excellent as it was. The menu at Red wasn't like any menu she'd ever seen before in a Mexican restaurant. It wasn't abnormally extensive, but the choices were far more varied and inventive than the budget-friendly restaurants she was used to. In the end, she'd depended on Drew to choose, and the spicy grilled tuna concoction had been nothing short of amazing.

"You're going to want at least a forkful. They serve it over some sort of flavored cake with a chocolate mole sauce." His smile was lazy and full of promise. "You'll think you've died and gone to heaven."

Considering the datelike quality of the evening, Deanna wasn't sure she hadn't already done so. But she shook her head ruefully. "Fine. A forkful only, though. I still need to be able to fit into my clothes when we go back to California."

In the flickering light of the candle that burned in the center of the table, Drew's gaze seemed warmer than ever as it glided over her. "I'm pretty sure you're safe," he murmured.

If they'd been back at the office in San Diego, his ball cap would have been turned backward and his eyes would have been full of all sorts of wicked.

Her fingers curled where they rested in her lap, safely hidden by the linen tablecloth on the table.

This is not a date. This is not a date.

She'd been repeating the mantra ever since Drew had opened the door of the low-slung sports car of J.R.'s that he'd borrowed for the evening. But the words were having even less effect now than they had then.

"I, um, am going to excuse myself for a quick moment," she finally said and started to push back the heavy chair that only seemed to make her more aware of her femininity, while making him look even more impossibly masculine.

He smoothly rose, though, and had pulled out her chair for her before she could so much as move it an inch.

He was wearing a crew-neck black sweater and the soft knit closely covering his wide shoulder was so close to her that she could have brushed her cheek against it.

She inhaled carefully as desire clutched inside her, hard and fast. Her legs felt shaky as she rose and stepped away from the table, trying to focus on the delectable aromas of food all around them and not on the delectable scent of him. "Thank you."

His smile was faint and she quickly turned away, only to nearly collide with a pretty waitress bearing a heavy tray toward the table next to them. But Drew's hand closed around Deanna's waist, scooping her aside, and the waitress smiled and shifted around her, continuing on her way without mishap.

"Okay?" Drew's word stirred the hair at her temple.

"Fine." If fine meant one who could hardly breathe. She took a step and his arm fell away and before she could do something really stupid, like pull it back around her, she headed much more carefully between the crowded tables until she reached the sanctuary of the ladies' room.

She ran her hot wrists under cool water at the hammered metal sink and looked sternly at her reflection.

Her eyes looked too wide for her face and color seemed to burn up her skin from the wide, low scooping neckline of the impossibly girly dress.

"This is not a date," she muttered.

"'Scuse me?" A striking, gray-haired woman wearing a mint's worth of turquoise jewelry stepped up to the sink beside her and smiled. "You all right, honey? You look a mite shaky."

Deanna nodded. "I'm fine."

"Handsome man waiting out there for you, I bet." She grinned. "That's what always gets me to feeling a little flustered."

Deanna managed an embarrassed smile. If it was obvious to a complete and utter stranger, then it would surely be like a neon light flashing in Drew's face.

"Just remember what my mama always told me." The woman plucked a folded paper towel off the stack of them sitting between the sinks. "Doesn't matter how much a man makes you breathless, darlin', any man worth his salt is gonna work darn hard to prove you make him feel the same way before he expects to go walking in your flower garden, if you know what I mean."

Despite herself, Deanna couldn't help but laugh. "Okay. Thanks for the advice."

"Then when he does come to smell those flowers o' yours, you knock his socks right off." The woman winked and sailed out the door.

Deanna gave a faint laugh again and turned off the water.

She dried her hands and smoothed down the full skirt of the butter-yellow dress that Isabella had loaned her.

She couldn't imagine ever knocking Drew's socks off, but it was certainly an intriguing image...

"This is not a date," she whispered again.

Feeling a little more controlled, she went back out to the dining room, only to find an older woman standing next to Drew, her hand on his shoulder as they laughed together.

They both seemed to notice Deanna at the same moment, and the woman—slightly shorter than Deanna, and far more curvaceous in her black slacks and ruffled red blouse—stepped forward and caught Deanna's hands in hers. "So this is the one to catch our Andrew's heart." With no hesitation at all, she leaned up and kissed Deanna's cheeks. "And no wonder. Such a beautiful girl."

Deanna couldn't help but smile in the face of the woman's infectious greeting.

"Deanna, this is Maria Mendoza," Drew introduced. "She and her husband, Jose, are the ones who founded this place."

"Sí, sí." Maria tucked her arm around

Deanna's waist and squeezed. "We have seen many romances come to fruition here at Red." Her dark eyes danced. "But I'm glad to see our Drew has beautiful company tonight, unlike the other evenings he's sat alone at the bar."

Deanna shot Drew a startled look.

He'd grabbed the woman's wrinkling hand and pulled her toward him to drop a noisy kiss on her cheek. "You were as much beautiful company as I could handle, Maria."

"Bah. Not even a devil like you can make my Jose jealous." She lightly slapped his hands and turned again to Deanna. "Andrew tells me how hard you work, *niña,* while he worries and searches for his father." She gave Drew a look. "That's a good woman to have by your side through life."

Drew's smile stayed in place, but Deanna wondered if Maria could see the shadows that entered his gaze as easily as she could.

"But enough of worrisome things." Maria clasped her hands together. "When is the wedding date?"

Deanna shot Drew a look. "We—"

"We haven't had a chance to set one," he said smoothly, and his gaze looked as clear as ever, making Deanna wonder if the shadows had been her imagination after all.

"But do you want a big wedding, or small…" Maria smiled, surprisingly impish for a woman who Deanna guessed was well into her seventies. "I never tire of weddings."

"Deanna doesn't like being the center of attention," Drew said, looking oddly serious.

"Ah." Maria nodded sagely. "A small, intimate affair, then. Or even an elopement?" She sighed happily. "So romantic." Then she waved at their seats. "Now, forgive an old woman and sit. Sit. Andrew wants me to bring out my flan for you, *niña.* You'll sit in the candlelight and feed each other and fall in love all over again." She squeezed Drew's cheeks, then Deanna's, and hurried through the tables, purpose in her steps.

Deanna blinked a little and slowly sat. "Wow."

"That's a good word to describe Maria." Drew took his own seat. "You could have told her we weren't really engaged. It's going to come out sooner or later, because my father's not coming back."

Deanna went still. Her unwise enjoyment of their not-a-date started to drain away. "You don't know that, Drew. You can't give up hope. Not yet."

"Can't I?" His gaze skewered hers. "What about any of this is giving you hope?"

He was talking about his father, but he might as well have been talking about them. She tried to clear the knot out of her throat and failed. "If that's the way you feel, then you…you could have corrected Maria yourself about—" She broke off and waved her hand. The diamond ring glittered in the candlelight. "Particularly because it seems you've been spending plenty of time here on your own."

His lips tightened. "I had to go somewhere." His voice was too low for anyone but her to hear.

"Why?" She lowered her voice, too, leaning toward him across the table. This, she knew, wasn't about his father. "Just to get away from me?"

"Yes."

Even though she'd expected exactly that answer, she still felt a hideous sting.

But at least now she had her answer.

The kiss they'd shared that afternoon that had rocked her existence had been from a man who'd simply needed comfort.

Even comfort from the likes of her.

She blinked hard, looking away from him. *This is definitely not a date.*

"Here we are." Maria returned, bearing a white plate with the beautifully presented custard dessert that she set between them with a beaming smile. She handed Deanna a sparkling silver spoon, and another to Drew. "Enjoy." With a sly smile, she quickly moved away from the table.

Deanna was afraid that if she put one spoon in her mouth she would be sick. But she was very aware of Maria watching from the sidelines and the delightful woman had done nothing to deserve being disappointed.

It wasn't Maria's fault that she—like everyone else—had all too easily believed the lie that she and Drew had perpetrated.

So Deanna dipped the tip of the spoon through the ruffles of whipped cream, glistening chocolate sauce and silky custard and tucked it into her mouth. Flavors exploded in her mouth and she forced a smile in Maria's direction. "Delicious."

Maria's eyebrows rose and she nodded, making her silver-streaked dark hair bounce around her shoulders. Her hands fluttered in an urging sort of way.

Deanna looked back at Drew. She scooped up another spoon of the confection and leaned across the table toward him. "Open up." Her voice was flat.

He slowly leaned closer, too, and put his lips around the spoon.

Her hand trembled violently and she quickly sat back in her chair, setting the spoon down on the linen tablecloth. "There. I had a bite. It's delicious. So can we go now?"

"I don't leave because I don't want to be around you." His voice was low, but deliberate. He slowly dipped his own spoon into the dessert. "I leave because I do. Too much."

The aching tightness at the back of her jaws went lax. Butterflies suddenly flitted around inside her chest. "Excuse me?"

He lifted the spoon and held it toward her. "Open."

She mindlessly parted her lips and leaned forward.

The cool silver spoon slipped past and just as mindlessly, she closed her lips softly over the tidbit.

He slowly withdrew the spoon. "Kind of tastes like flowers, doesn't it?"

A shiver worked down her spine. "Flowers?"

"Whatever stuff it is that Maria refuses to say is in her recipe." He scooped a spoonful into his mouth and his hooded eyes narrowed for a moment in appreciation.

Deanna swallowed, her mouth running dry. Her hands curled around the heavy, carved arms of her chair.

"Not that I know what a flower really tastes like," he continued, dipping the spoon yet again before extending it toward her. "But that's what I can't help thinking every time I put my mouth around it."

"Flowers," she murmured huskily.

His dimple flirted next to the faint smile on his lips. "A whole damn garden of 'em."

She exhaled and leaned forward, parting her lips for another bite.

Chapter 11

"That's going to be one lucky baby coming into the world with you two as parents." Drew lifted his wineglass in a toast toward Isabella and J.R. who were standing arm in arm in front of the fireplace where a low fire was crackling with a comfortable warmth.

"Hear, hear," Jeremy echoed.

They, along with Lily and the rest of their brothers and their wives, had gathered in the great room at Molly's Pride later that week to celebrate the coming baby.

They could easily have included more of the family, but Isabella had persuaded J.R. to keep things small. "We'll have even more to celebrate with everyone when your father returns," she'd told him.

Now, as she watched the family mingle, Deanna fervently hoped that the Fortune and Mendoza families would have that opportunity. Unfortunately, judging from the expressions on some of the faces there, she knew that after two weeks since their father had gone missing, at least some of them—Drew particularly—were seriously doubting whether that day would come.

Not that Drew had said anything more than he had that evening at Red. Not that Drew had done anything more than what he'd done that evening at Red, either.

She was torn between wanting to comfort and encourage him to have more faith where his father was concerned—even though she had her own painful doubts after all this time—and wanting to kick herself for continuing to fall into his allure when she ought to know better. And in the end, all she seemed capable of doing was walking on eggshells around him whenever they were alone.

Which, thanks to his admittedly valid excuse of hunting down leads over his missing father, were increasingly rare.

She shook her head when Nick passed by

with another wine bottle and lifted her glass, which was still nearly full. Everyone had a glass. Even Isabella, though hers was filled with fruit juice.

Bethany sank onto the couch next to where Deanna sat. "Darr told me that you went with Drew and Ross to see the car when they first learned about it." She kept her voice low, sliding a glance toward Lily, who was standing near the windows with Drew and Jeremy. "I don't think I could have stood to see it. It must have been so disturbing."

"It was." In so many more ways than Deanna could share with anyone, except Drew. And especially Drew. "The, uh, the car's in a very remote location," she added, trying to focus on the conversation at hand, and not the subject of her thoughts who was looking terribly solemn as he stood with his father's fiancée, his half-empty wineglass dangling from his long fingers.

Charlene joined them, perching on the arm of the couch. She'd obviously overheard. "The guys are all going back tomorrow. They're going to take some climbing equipment and do a more extensive search. Try to reach the areas where the search dogs couldn't go."

Deanna's gaze sought out Drew again. He

was wearing an oatmeal-colored shirt that she knew wasn't his and blue jeans that she knew were and his dark hair was brushed severely back from his face. Even from across the room she could see his pensive expression that didn't quite fit what was supposed to be a celebration.

She could hardly envision another search of the accident site, much less imagine Drew wanting to return there. If they found William in an area even less accessible, they surely wouldn't be finding him alive.

And maybe Bethany and Charlene were thinking the same thing because neither one of them pursued the topic any further. Instead, they all looked over to where J.R. was still holding Isabella close against his side.

"I love the idea of another baby," Charlene said, grinning a little. She was obviously determined to find a more cheerful subject. "Particularly one that I don't have to be pregnant with just yet."

Bethany laughed softly. "I wouldn't mind it so much, though it would probably be wiser to wait until Randi's through her terrorizing twos. What about you, Deanna? Do you and Drew plan to have kids right away or wait a while?"

Startled, Deanna's gaze finally broke away from Drew, but she could only stare at the other woman. She couldn't come up with an appropriate response to save her soul.

"Knowing Drew, I'll bet he wants to hold off on that," Charlene inserted, seemingly unaware of Deanna's tied tongue.

Bethany nodded knowingly. "But then, we figured Drew was going to hold off forever on getting married. Turns out we didn't know as much as we thought we did. So…?" She turned her bright gaze back to Deanna.

"I… I would like to have children," she finally managed. She was miserably afraid that her cheeks were red, even though she hadn't technically lied.

"Just not right away," Bethany guessed helpfully. Her eyes sparkled with merriment.

"Settling into married life is pretty fun," Charlene agreed. "If you know what I mean."

Deanna smiled weakly as the other two women laughed.

"Mind if I steal my fiancée?" Drew suddenly appeared, leaning over them from behind the couch.

Deanna quickly slid off the couch and smoothed down the gauzy white skirt that was another loaner from Isabella. She didn't know what Drew wanted, but she was almost pathetically grateful for the interruption, despite the fear that she could very well be jumping from the fat into the fire.

And when he wrapped his hand around hers as they left the room, that fear deepened even more.

It wasn't fear of him. Just the knowledge that—where Drew was concerned—she was totally out of her depth.

Since he'd—intentionally or not—left her feeling practically seduced over Maria Mendoza's flan at Red, he hadn't so much as touched her. Nor had he changed his ways when it came to sharing the bed in their guest room.

He didn't say a word now either, as he drew her through the house, only stopping once as they went through the laundry room, to hook a jacket off one of the pegs near the back door.

"It's cold." He finally let go of her hand, only to push the jacket into it as he ushered her outside.

Her teeth were in danger of chattering, but it wasn't the chilly night air that was the cause. Nevertheless, she managed to tug the somewhat stiff, woven coat around the shoulders of the loose-knit blouse without fumbling with it too badly. "What's wrong?"

"Nothing. I just wanted some air." He made a low sound and grabbed the lapels of the jacket and pulled them close beneath her chin. "Judging by your expression in there, I thought you looked about like I felt." He headed down the shallow steps away from the house and the warm glow of light. "What were you all talking about anyway?"

She chewed her lip and followed. "They wanted to know if we were planning on having children right away or if we wanted to wait a while." She hoped the darkness did a better job of hiding her hot cheeks than it did the surprise in his expression as he looked back at her.

"And what did you tell them?"

"What does it matter? None of it's real anyway."

"Maybe I'm curious."

She let out a huff and lifted her hands. "Fine. I told them the truth. That, yes, *I* would like to have children someday. Obviously, I wasn't answering for you." The low heel of the tall boots she'd borrowed from Isabella caught slightly in the ground and Drew's arm shot out, catching her shoulder.

"Watch your step."

She was trying to. Literally and metaphorically. "Thanks," she mumbled and continued walking, grateful when his hand fell away. "What were you and Jeremy talking about with Lily?"

"What does it matter?"

"Maybe I'm curious," she returned pointedly.

He exhaled noisily. "I was apologizing to her, okay? For being such an ass about everything when she and my father got involved."

Her footsteps halted. "You apologized?"

He stopped, too. "You think I'm incapable of it or something?"

"No, of course not. I'm just—"

"—surprised."

"Yes. And glad." Maybe he'd stop torturing himself so much over what couldn't be changed.

He made a low sound that could have meant anything. "She said that it would mean a lot to my father that we were all here in Red Rock. Supporting her. Supporting each other." His lips twisted slightly. "She said how much he loved us all. How proud he was of us." Her heart ached when his voice went rough.

"She knew about the picture," he added after a moment. "The one of my mother. Jeremy told her I'd found it. But she already knew that Dad always kept it in his sun visor." He cleared his throat abruptly. "She said she knew how much my mother meant to him because that's how she felt about Ryan and it's one of the reasons she loves Dad as much as she does. Loves. Present tense." He shook his head. "She hasn't lost hope at all."

While Drew was losing more by the day. Deanna pushed her hands in the pockets of her jacket before they could reach for him. "I'm glad you talked with her," she said again.

"She also said that it means a lot to her that Jeremy and I have stayed in Red Rock."

"I'm sure it would."

He started walking again. "Since when have you wanted kids?"

Despite the aching wish that she could take away some of his pain, she felt herself bristle. "Why wouldn't I? Not everyone is phobic about such things like you are and it's a pretty average desire." They were nearing one of the barns and Drew's hand touched the small of her back, directing her around the side of it where the smell of mowed grass was strong, even at that hour.

"I never said I had a phobia about kids."

"Are you saying you'd like to have them?" Disbelief dripped from her voice.

"I never didn't want them. But kids are better off when they're raised by married parents. I know that's not the way a lot of families are now, but it's still what I believe."

Thoroughly nonplussed, she lifted her eyebrows, trying to hide it. "And since marriage is one of your phobias…"

"Our marriage excluded, of course," he said wryly.

How easily he could be wry while she felt wholly off balance. But she managed a shrug and a casual "of course."

At the rate things had gone since William disappeared, she couldn't envision their "engagement" ever reaching an altar-bound conclusion anyway. She felt certain that he was thinking the same thing, particularly after their dinner at Red.

"I just never heard you talk about wanting kids before," he added.

She couldn't fathom where his sudden interest had come from.

He was so much easier to deal with when he behaved exactly the way she expected.

No surprises.

But all he'd been since they'd arrived in Texas was one tall, disturbing, heart-wrenching surprise.

She clutched the jacket more closely around her, willing away a shiver, and quickened her step even more.

Maybe he just wanted to focus on something other than his father and his conversation with Lily. "It's not as if I spend my entire day at the office talking about my personal wishes and aspirations," she pointed out.

"No. Until New Year's Eve, you barely acted as if you had any desires outside of work at all."

She had one overriding desire, and considering everything, he had to know by now as well as she did that he was it. "Personal lives should have no place in the workplace."

"So says Gigi's daughter." He caught her shoulder again, halting her forward momentum. "Your mother has been all about being personal in the workplace, so you've gone to the opposite extreme."

There was no point in denying the truth. Particularly because he knew about her mother now, too. She crossed her arms over her chest. She couldn't imagine why he'd have an issue over her practice. Aside from his penchant for dating money-hungry bimbos that he enlisted her aid when it was time to send them on their way, he didn't really bring much of his truly personal life into the office, either. "I don't imagine that you'd want it otherwise. The thing you like best about me is that I'm a focused assistant."

So focused and dedicated in fact, she thought hopelessly, that he'd figured she'd happily disappear back into the woodwork where she'd always been once his need of her as his convenient wife was over.

He let out a faint sound caught somewhere between a laugh and a cough. "Don't be so certain that you know what I like best about you."

Which had her shivering all over again.

She might as well be a pendulum of emotion where he was concerned, swinging from one end of the spectrum to the other. And she couldn't seem to do one thing about it but stay here in Red Rock with him even when she figured that the only reason he hadn't sent her away by now was because he "appreciated" the work she'd been doing on his behalf for Fortune Forecasting.

His hand was still curving around her shoulder, adding fuel to her agitation. She shifted from one foot to the other, and tightened her folded arms.

His hand still didn't fall away.

And despite the moonlight, his hooded gaze was making her distinctly edgy. She wasn't sure her heart could take another episode of wondering if she was misinterpreting every move he made. Everything he said.

She sucked in her lower lip for a second. "Charlene said that all of you are going back to the accident site tomorrow with hiking equipment and searching the area more."

He nodded.

"You're really going to go with them?"

He nodded again. "Yes."

"Are you sure you want to?" Hadn't he seen enough of the devastation for one lifetime?

"The only thing I'm sure about right now is that I want to sleep with you."

The world felt as if it came to a screeching halt. Everything inside her went still. She stared at him.

His hand slowly, deliberately, slid over her shoulder until the warm tips of his fingers delved beneath the jacket collar to graze her skin. "Cat got your tongue?"

"Evidently." Her voice was faint. There was no danger of misinterpreting now, and she was hardly able to think past the blood suddenly thundering through her veins.

His thumb roved up and down the side of

her bare neck. "Problem is, I don't want to complicate things."

She barely kept from arching her neck against his touch like a greedy cat seeking more. "It's already complicated." More complicated than he would ever suspect, at least where her heart was concerned. "That's what happens when you get mired in a lie."

His hand slid a little until his thumb found the pulse at the base of her throat.

"Yeah." His voice was deep as he pressed his thumb against her pulse with enough pressure to let them both know how rapidly it was beating. "But this isn't a lie."

She'd been sleeping—more or less—beside him for two weeks. But in that moment, the feel of her heartbeat throbbing beneath the warm pad of this thumb was so much more intensely intimate than anything that had gone before that she was in danger of dissolving into a puddle right there where they stood in the moonlit shadows of the barn.

"Drew—"

"What *would* be a lie would be continuing to pretend that I don't want to make love to you."

She pulled in a shaking breath and didn't even care just then that it sounded as openly desperate as she felt. "It's…it's the situation. If your father weren't missing, you—"

"—would still want this. Bringing you with me to Red Rock just brought it home to me." His thumb stroked up her throat until it reached her chin. He gently pushed upward, stilling her shaking head and the denial of his words. "Look at me."

She couldn't do anything but.

"You have to know by now that I can't get through the day without wanting you," he said, and even though her emotions quaked, she recognized that he sounded more grim than romantic. "And I damn sure can't get through another night. But I don't want to ruin a good thing either, and the last thing I want—when this is all over—is for you to run for the hills."

Of course he was already anticipating an "over."

Her stomach knotted. The fastest way any woman in Drew's life could lose his interest was to let him know they were falling for him. Deanna had seen it happen over and over again. And even though she didn't want to categorize herself with any of those women, she knew that she was no different.

If Drew learned how she felt, *really* felt, he'd forget all about the "good thing" they had

going. Maybe—given their working relationship—he'd feel some compunction when he
ultimately showed her the door, but she had
absolutely no doubt that the door was where
she would be destined.

He'd find himself another assistant.

And she'd find herself out of his life in
every way.

What was worse? Staying with him while
hiding her true feelings, or being without him
because she hadn't?

Whichever path she took was paved with
misery.

All she had to do was tell him that they
could become lovers and nothing would
change, and she'd at least have some part of
him.

Was that how her mother thought, when she
fell for her unattainable suitors?

Maybe Gigi wasn't so hard to understand
after all.

Maybe, in comparison to her mother's head-
long rushing into impossible relationships,
Deanna was the real coward.

She moistened her lips. Swallowed. Her fingers pressed into the sinewy strength of his
forearms. "I don't want to ruin anything, either."

"So where does that leave us?"

"I don't know." Her voice was nearly soundless.

He exhaled roughly and stepped closer. "I need a better answer, Dee. Tell me no. Better yet, tell me hell, no. And I'll somehow figure out a way to get this under control."

"Oh, sure." She moved her hands to his chest and shoved against him, but he was immovable. "Make me be the bad guy."

"Not bad. Just stronger than I am." His hands slid behind her. Found the small of her back and deliberately urged her against him. "And you're definitely not a guy."

While he most definitely *was*.

Her fingers were suddenly curling into his chest, rather than trying to push. He'd made certain that she wore a jacket against the evening chill, but he was only in his shirtsleeves. Nevertheless, her fingers felt scorched by his heat, even through the nubby silk of his shirt.

"I don't know what to make of you," she whispered. "At Red you were—" She broke off, unable to describe what had transpired that night. "But since then—" Again she broke off, just as stuck.

And here she was supposed to be good with words.

"I know." His voice was even. "I'm the worst kind of bastard. But know this, there has barely been a minute in a single day since we came to Red Rock when I haven't thought about you. About us."

Her heart squeezed. His words sent shocking thrills straight through her.

"I should tell you no," she whispered. For both their sakes.

He claimed that he couldn't say no himself. And even though she was painfully aware that he wasn't making any professions of love, rather than frightening her off, knowing that he couldn't deny he wanted her any longer made her feel more than a little bold.

And she could feel the way he was suddenly holding himself stiffly.

As if he'd braced for rejection.

She fisted the silk shirt and levered onto the toes of her borrowed boots until her lips hovered close to his. "I should say no," she whispered again. "But I can't make myself do it."

No matter what that meant for her—for their—future.

He exhaled and she tasted his warm breath on her lips.

Then his arms tightened around her, practically lifting her right off her toes as he pulled her even closer. His mouth covered hers, and whatever doubts that might have lingered about the wisdom of their actions died an unobtrusive death beneath the brilliance of his kiss.

If it seemed as if the world had stopped spinning before, now it whirled.

Madly.

Her head felt as though it was spinning, and her heart felt like it would burst out of her chest. All she could do was hang on to the only thing that might keep her sane. Him.

Her mouth opened under his plundering kiss, her hands curled into his hair. And the world spun even more dizzily.

His mouth dragged over her cheek, her temple. "Push the door."

It took a moment for her brain to make sense out of his low growl. And a moment after that for her vision to see anything beyond his face.

But then she realized he'd lifted her into his arms and carried her around to the front of the barn doors.

No wonder she was spinning.

She stretched out an arm and gave the door a push. Despite the rustic look of it, the door smoothly slid open a foot and without a second's hesitation, Drew turned her sideways and carried her into the dark warmth.

"Do you know where you're going?"

"Heaven." He lowered her legs until her feet hit the ground and then he was stepping closer to her, brushing right up against her until the barn door at her back stopped them. "And no, I can't see a bloody damn thing. So unless you want to take a stroll back to the house right now—"

"No." She shook her head even though he couldn't possibly see. Not even the door that was still ajar let in any light. She couldn't even see him standing in front of her and he was so close she could feel the rise and fall of his chest against her cheek. If they went back to the house, it would give her time to chicken out; to start thinking with her head again, instead of her heart.

And if she did that, she just might hate herself forever...

His hands pushed beneath the jacket until it fell off her shoulders. "Good. Because I don't want to wait, and I can feel everything I want to." Unerringly, his palms closed over her hips, then purposefully delved beneath the loosely knit top.

Desire clenched hard inside her and she bit

down on her tongue to keep from gasping, but a faint, mewling sound still escaped.

"We're in a barn," he murmured, his lips touching her temple. "Don't hold back."

Her hands instinctively closed around his arms. "A-are there animals in here or something?" She couldn't hear anything but the thundering of her heartbeat in her head and the rustle of her skirt against the solid wood behind her back.

"Just me."

Her head fell back against the door as his hands slipped over her waist, climbing toward her breasts. "You're not an animal."

"You're not wearing a bra," he murmured, quickly discovering that particular fact for himself. "Makes me feel like an animal."

Her lips parted. She hauled in oxygen as his hands slowly shaped her breasts as if he were molding a sculpture. Only she could feel her flesh tightening, swelling, and no inanimate sculpture ever did that. Not even beneath the chisel of the most skilled artisan.

Then his fingers dragged over her aching nipples, taunting them to even harder peaks, and she couldn't stop the moan from rising in her throat. She stared up at him in the utter darkness, feeling his touch, feeling his heat, but not being able to see.

It was as disturbingly intense as the feel of his thumb had been on the pulse at the base of her throat.

Intense. Erotic. And emboldening.

She exhaled and the shaking sound of her breath sounded loud between them. Her hands slid over his forearms until they reached his wrists. They felt bony. Strong. And as her fingers explored them, she realized she could feel *his* pulse charging beneath her fingertips, too.

"Maybe there are two animals here," she whispered. Her fingers grazed past his wrists, over the backs of his hands that cupped her breasts and she pressed her palms against them. Her fingers slid between his. "Harder."

She felt his momentary stillness, then his hands tightened on her and the shards of light pulsing through her blood went even brighter, aiming straight to the center of her. Then she heard rustling again, felt his movement, and his hands moved beneath hers and she felt the wet heat of his mouth close over her breast.

She gasped. His other hand pushed at her sweater where it was tangling beneath her arms. "Take it off."

Shaking, she obediently dragged it over her

head, not feeling the slightest worry for where it landed—or what it might be landing in.

She was a California girl. She didn't know barns from nothing. All she knew, right then, was that Drew was sending *her* straight to heaven and he wasn't stopping to ask directions.

Her head fell back against the door again when his mouth slowly dragged down the valley between her breasts, over her stomach, not even pausing when he reached the stretchy waist of the gauzy skirt. He just pulled it down as he went. "If you're as naked under this as you were the sweater, I'm going to have a heart attack," he muttered.

She gave a strangled laugh. "No." Her fingers slid through his hair. She'd never realized how silky or thick it was. "I'm not that hard-up for clothes." But she'd rinsed out her bra after her shower and it was still damp, hanging safely hidden in the guest room's closet where she'd thought Drew wouldn't be able to notice it.

"On second thought, that might be a shame," he drawled and she nearly jumped when she felt his lips graze her right hip. Then he was tugging the skirt down even more. She felt it pass her thighs, then her knees. "Lift." His hand circled her right knee.

She lifted and felt him pull the skirt over her boot. Her hand tightened against his shoulder as she lifted her left. And then the skirt was gone.

And even though the barn was perfectly warm, she felt chills dance over her skin. Aside from panties and leather boots, she was nude. She twisted her fingers in the fabric of his shirt. "You take something off, too."

"Honey, before we're through there won't be anything but skin between us." His hands circled behind her knees again and she felt his lips against the front of her thigh while those hands started to slowly climb. Higher and higher while he maddened her with a kiss on her leg here, then there, never in any path or order.

And then his hands reached her derriere, and she felt his fingers slowly explore the narrow bands of stretchy lace that masqueraded as panties. "If I'd only known—" his voice was low and deliciously rough "—that under those ugly suits you wore stuff straight out of a man's fantasy, I'd have never gotten anything done at the office."

She felt herself flush, but this time, it was a good flush. "I like pretty things."

"Yeah, I noticed that when I saw the things you'd unpacked in the drawer that first day when you lost the towel." His fingers hooked the lace, teasingly gliding back and forth against her hip.

"If you were a gentleman you wouldn't remind me."

"Baby, I'm a man, and that was a pretty spectacular moment for me. See, I like pretty things, too," he murmured meaningfully. "And I've been thinking about you wearing them... and then not wearing them...ever since." He continued tracing along the edges of the lace across her abdomen. Then lower.

She sucked in a breath. "Wh-what are you doing?"

"What do you think?" He waited a beat. "What do you *want?*"

For him to end this wondrous torture. "I want you."

His fingers delved between her thighs and his voice dropped a notch. "So I can feel." His fingers glided over the damp lace, then retraced his steps. Again. And again.

She made a strangled sound. "Drew—"

"So perfect," he murmured, his breath hot against her thigh. "So wet."

She had a strange sense that she ought to have been mortified. "I can't help it," she admitted breathlessly. "That's what you do to me."

"Since when?"

She blessed the pitch darkness because it blacked out inhibition. And cursed it for the very same reason. "Since always."

He drew in an audible breath that made her nerves knot even more. His palm slowly cupped her through the clinging lace. "Have you thought about us? Like this?"

He was killing her by degrees. All she had to do was deny it and keep some bit of herself protected.

She moistened her lips. Kneaded her fingers against his head. "Yes." Her admission whispered through the darkness.

He made a low, hissing sound and then he was dragging the lace aside and she cried out loud as his lips found her bare, wet flesh.

Her legs nearly gave way as flames engulfed her, driving her straight up a shuddering, quaking peak.

She was still shaking when he finally straightened and she heard the rustle of his clothes. And then his hands slid behind her thighs, lifting her legs, and she cried out again as he sank into her.

No artifice. No pretense.

He was just Drew. The man she loved.

And then he uttered her name in a rough voice and she closed her eyes against the darkness as he carried them both straight to heaven.

Chapter 12

"Morning." J.R. looked up when Drew headed into the kitchen early the next morning. "You're up early."

Drew managed a grunt and headed straight for the coffeepot that his brother had already brewed. He had no intentions of telling J.R. why he was up a good hour earlier than they'd agreed upon.

Not when he wasn't ready to recognize the reason himself.

He'd made love to his assistant in a damn barn, thinking stupidly that it wouldn't ruin things. Wouldn't change things.

Maybe for Deanna it hadn't.

But the second he'd sunk into her and lost his mind in a way that he'd never lost it before, he'd known he was in serious trouble.

Trouble of the kind he'd vowed to stay away from since he'd found his bride-of-weeks screwing the hell out of his best man.

So he pulled out a mug and started pouring some coffee. "Best we get an early start, isn't it? It's not every day we head out for a hike to find our father's body."

J.R. grimaced. "Hell, Drew. I'm hoping to hell that's not the case."

"And I can't stop feeling that it is." He slammed back a mouthful of java even though it singed all the way down. "Darr's meeting us over at Nick's place with all the hiking gear?"

J.R. looked as though he wanted to say something, but then he nodded. "Then we'll pick up Jeremy at the Double Crown on our way out of town." He poured the rest of the coffeepot into a thermos and capped it before grabbing the sturdy canvas backpack that sat on a bar stool. "Isabella packed us food last night. But you've got time to eat some breakfast before we meet up with them." He nodded toward the thickly sliced ham that was sitting on the counter where he'd obviously made himself a sandwich for his own breakfast.

The last thing Drew had on his mind was food. But he knew they were in for a long trek and he put together a sandwich, too, that he wrapped in a napkin while J.R. stowed the makings back in the refrigerator. "Might as well get going," he said. "Darr's always early. He'll be at Nick's already."

J.R. nodded. He looked no more anxious for the task than Drew felt, and they quietly let themselves out of the house. J.R.'s truck was parked near the back door and they headed for it. "Where'd you and Deanna disappear to last night anyway?"

Drew managed not to choke on the mouthful of homemade bread and salty ham. "Just took a walk," he mumbled around the food that he had to wash down with another blistering hot gulp of coffee from the mug he'd carried along. He ignored the sidelong look J.R. gave him and stretched his legs out in the truck as he forced himself to take another bite of the sandwich and after a moment, J.R. started up the truck.

"You know, she's the smartest thing you've ever done."

Drew inhaled a piece of bread and sat forward, coughing hard. J.R. reached across the wide cab and slapped him hard on the back.

Drew lifted his hand. "I'm fine," he muttered.

"Except you're as antsy as a damn cat," J.R. pointed out. "What the hell's wrong with you? You and Deanna have a fight or something?"

"No." His jaws clamped together.

J.R. shook his head. "You always were the most cussed, stubborn one of us."

"No. That would've been Darr or Jeremy. Otherwise they'd have gone into business with Dad, too."

J.R. gave a short laugh. "Yeah. Maybe so." He put the truck in motion and the headlights of his truck cut through the still, early morning, casting a wide arch over the hacienda as he smoothly backed away.

It was a damn thing to think that going on this hike—and finding whatever the hell they were destined to find—was preferable to thinking about facing Deanna.

Drew knew he'd left her confused.

Hell, he was confused.

After the most singularly erotic, mind-blowing sex he'd ever had in his life, they'd dressed and returned to the then-silent house and headed to their bedroom.

And in the soft light that had pooled over the inviting bed and turned Deanna's green eyes to emerald as she'd shyly looked at him, clearly expecting something—a kiss, a word, a touch—he'd been terrified.

Terrified of getting into bed with her. Terrified of touching her. Terrified of not touching her.

So he'd made some fool excuse about getting himself a nightcap, and he'd walked out of the room. Same as he'd been keeping away from that room as much as humanly possible since they'd arrived.

Only this time, he knew his actions weren't forgivable.

Not after what had transpired in the barn solely because of him.

He'd never been able to satisfy any woman who mattered to him. Not his quickly ex-wife. According to Drew's father, not his own mother, either. And last night, he'd hurt the last person on earth who'd deserved it.

Deanna.

He realized that J.R. had stopped the truck again, this time in front of the barn.

The barn.

"Gotta grab some rope," his brother said as he got out of the truck. He strode over to the barn and shoved open the door.

Drew looked away.

He didn't need to look at the barn.

The memories of what had occurred there were indelibly engraved on his damned soul.

He was gone.

Again.

Deanna rolled onto her back on the mattress and looked at the pillow beside hers. There was a faint indentation left from Drew's head when he'd briefly slept there. But considering the distance that had started yawning between them the second they'd left the blissful sanctuary of darkness the barn had provided, he might as well have never been in the same bed with her at all.

She tossed her arm over her stinging eyes.

What had she hoped for?

That Drew would suddenly realize that he loved her?

That just because she'd let him into her body as well as her heart, he'd feel the same?

Hot tears leaked from beneath her tightly closed eyes.

It didn't matter that she knew he was going back to the accident site with his brothers. She still felt abandoned. She'd felt abandoned when he'd all but raced out of the bedroom the night before when they'd returned from the barn.

And it suddenly felt untenable to lie in the bed that they could have shared so much more meaningfully, and she slid off the mattress and numbly went into the bathroom.

Only there, instead of the reflection of a well-loved woman, the person looking back at her through the bathroom mirror just looked… broken.

She looked like her mother.

Her mother who was, for all of her faults, alive and well while Drew and his brothers couldn't be certain of any such thing where their father was concerned.

Deanna exhaled slowly and turned away from her reflection.

She went back into the bedroom, unearthed her cell phone from the depths of her purse and turned it on. She was a little surprised that the battery was still holding a charge since she'd forgotten to bring the charger with her to Red Rock. And even though it was still early in the morning in Texas—and two hours earlier in California—she dialed her mother's house.

After only a single ring, though, Gigi's sleepy voice—sharp with alarm—answered. "Deedee, what's wrong?"

"Nothing." Everything.

"You're calling me at—" she heard muffled movements "—four in the morning and nothing is wrong?"

Deanna sank onto the foot of the bed and eyed herself in the tall, slanted mirror across from her. "Mom, did you ever keep a baby book from when I was a baby?"

"Of course I did. It's in the attic in the trunk along with your baptism dress from when you were six months old and my mother's wedding dress that your crumb of a father never gave me a chance to wear." Alarm had morphed into impatience. "Deanna, what is *wrong?* You never call me like this."

She pinched the bridge of her nose and looked away from her reflection. Considering the piles of possessions that her mother had amassed, she was stunned that Gigi knew the whereabouts of anything. Much less the fact that she'd been so wrong about the baby book in the first place. And her baptism dress? Church hadn't been part of her childhood and she couldn't recall Gigi ever talking about it.

But then maybe her mother had had her reasons. Different reasons than the basic lack of interest that Deanna had grown up believing.

"Nothing's wrong," she insisted. "I just wanted to know, that's all." She heard her mother's sigh. And then she went stock-still when she heard the murmur of a low, deep voice in the background. A man's voice. "Gigi, do you have someone there with you?"

"Just a minute." Deanna heard more rustling. "All right. I'm in the kitchen now." Gigi's voice was much less hushed. "You've messed things up with that honey of a boss of yours, haven't you? Is that why you're calling me in the middle of the night? If you want me to tell you how to fix things, just say so."

Was it disappointment sinking through her? Disillusionment? Or maybe it was just finally acceptance of the fact that Gigi would always be... Gigi. For good or bad.

"No, I don't need anything fixed," she said quietly. You couldn't fix a broken heart, could you? "I just wanted to hear your voice." Which was, she also realized, the absolute truth. "I'm sorry it's so early."

She heard Gigi sigh noisily. "Well, it is that. I'm not sure what Frank is going to think, considering the hour. It's not as if this is an emergency or anything, is it?"

"No. No emergency." Deanna propped her elbows on her knees, cupping the phone to her ear. That would imply something sudden, and there was nothing sudden about loving Drew and not being loved back. "Frank is presumably the voice I heard in the background?"

Gigi's voice suddenly turned girlish. "He's wonderful, Deedee. You see, I got another job. I tried to tell you this past week, but you haven't returned any of my messages."

"A job." She managed a smile. "That's great. Where at?"

"A law firm, naturally. Horne, Hollings, and Howard. Up in Escondido." The town was on the northern side of San Diego.

Deanna tried not to wince. Gigi was a legal secretary. Deanna couldn't exactly be surprised that her mother kept going back to it even if Deanna kept hoping that Gigi would break her pattern at least once. "I guess that's where you met Frank?"

"Oh, good heavens, no. Everyone who works at Triple H are women. No. I met *Frank* at the counselor's office. Don't you listen to any of my messages?"

Deanna sat up straight. "You've been going to the counselor?"

"Well, I told your boss I would when he called because *you* wouldn't talk to me." Gigi sounded miffed again.

"What?" Deanna's voice went sharp. "Drew called you? When?"

"It was last week sometime. After you left me that completely unfeeling message. I've been to two appointments now."

Deanna swallowed. She was far more unnerved by Drew's actions than by her mother's chastisement. He'd told her they would handle her mother together. She hadn't believed it at the time, even if it had sounded wholly appealing.

Turns out, he'd handled it all. And succeeded where she'd failed.

Her hand shook and she pressed the phone harder against her ear. "That's really great, Mom." And it was. Even beyond her shock, she recognized that. "So, you met Frank there?" Was he another patient, or—heaven forbid—the counselor? She dreaded asking.

"Oh, he's wonderful, Deedee. I know you'll like him. He's so sensible. Just like you. He has his own business, you see. He's a plant expert, if you can believe that. Goes around putting in and taking care of the interior plants all around hundreds of office buildings in San Diego. He just takes care of every little thing." Gigi giggled. "Even me. And he's even helped me return the last four orders I received from the shopping channel. Wasn't that the sweetest thing?"

"Yes. That sounds very sweet."

"All right, well, since nothing's wrong, I'm going to go back to bed now. Frank gets up early, you see." She giggled again. "He has a lot of energy, if you know what I mean."

Deanna was torn between a groan and a reluctant laugh. "Okay, Mom."

"Deedee, you know how old it makes me feel to be called Mom."

"Sorry." Deanna exhaled. "I'll talk with you in a week or so, okay?"

"Whenever you like," Gigi chirped. "At least now you know my news. And I hope to heaven that you're making good use of your time with your boss. Girls like you can't afford not to make a good catch. Remember that."

Deanna grimaced. "I'll keep that in mind."

But her mother had already ended the call.

Deanna slowly lowered the phone. The battery bar was dwindling and she turned off the power again. And then, because she still couldn't bear to linger in the bedroom a moment longer, she took a brisk shower, pulled on her running gear and quietly let herself out of the hacienda.

She hadn't been able to outrun her emotions since they'd arrived in Texas. She knew that this morning would be no different.

Moving automatically, she stretched and started out slowly. But as she neared the barn, she picked up her pace and didn't slow once. Not even when tears started burning their way down her cheeks.

She ran until she couldn't run anymore and finally walked her way back to the hacienda. It took two hours.

But at least she wasn't crying anymore.

Because she knew that running around Molly's Pride trying to get over Drew Fortune was not going to get her anywhere. She'd fallen in love with a man who refused to be loved.

And now, it was time to go home.

The bedroom door was ajar when Drew went inside the house after he and J.R. got back to Molly's Pride that evening, and he wearily pushed it open, blindly heading inside.

The sight of Deanna's hard-sided suitcase sitting open on top of the neatly made bed had him stopping short, though. And the sight of her turning away from the closet, with that sexy pink dress she'd worn the day his father disappeared made everything else inside him seem to stop working, too.

Her gaze shied away from him as she moved to the suitcase. She was wearing that shapeless green sweater and jeans that she'd worn when they'd flown to Red Rock. "I didn't realize you were back."

He slowly closed the door. "Going somewhere?"

Her head ducked and her glossy red hair swung down to cover her cheek. "It's become quite clear that it's past time." She pulled the dress off the hanger and folded it inside the suitcase. "How did the search go?"

The only thing he and his brothers had found beyond the accident site were more rocks, more trees and more nothing.

"We didn't find his body," he said bluntly.

She inhaled sharply and looked at him. Probably for the first time since he'd walked out of their bedroom after "the barn."

She looked as miserable as he felt. Her eyes were bloodshot, her nose pink. "Is *that* what you hoped to find?"

Had he? Or had he been hoping like hell that they wouldn't, because then maybe he could put a cork into his certainty that his father was never coming back?

"You've been crying."

Her lashes fell and she turned back to fuss with her suitcase. Moving the zippered case of her cosmetics from one corner to the other, then back again. "No."

"You're a rotten liar."

"And yet you chose me to lie about—" she waved her arm encompassing the bedroom and the two of them *"—us."* Her lips twisted as she flipped the suitcase closed. "Guess that was a mistake on both our parts." She pushed the old-fashioned latches and they snapped closed with a sharp sound.

"Why now?"

She didn't look at him. "I have a life to get back to."

Since his father went missing, Drew knew that he'd barely given any consideration to the difficulties in Deanna's life. Not the ones she'd left behind, nor the ones created by her presence in Texas.

And even though he'd spent the better part of the last day reminding himself of all the reasons he was better off without her, the sight of her ready to leave now sent every one of those reasons scattering just as wildly as the rocks that had scattered beneath his hiking boots while he'd climbed over one ravine after another, hunting for any sign of his father.

"What were you planning to do? Sneak out before I got back?"

She shook her head. "I wouldn't have done that."

"Looks to me like you were." He moved into the room and as he did, she moved, too, keeping several feet of space between them.

He bit back a sigh. "I'm not going to jump you, for God's sake."

Her cheeks went red. "I never assumed that you would," she assured witheringly. She continued to the opened closet and retrieved her tennis shoes. Then she sat down on the side of the bed and began to pull them on.

Her gaze followed him warily when he dragged the chair from the corner, positioned it in front of her and sat down.

He'd learned, over and over again, that the quickest way to get through Deanna's reserve was to get into her personal space. Considering everything, that had become just as much a curse as a useful tool, though. And now was no exception.

He leaned toward her. "I shouldn't have acted the way I did."

She jerked the laces of her shoe into a lopsided bow. "I don't know what you mean."

He just looked at her.

"Fine. You shouldn't have. And I should have known better than to expect otherwise."

Her lips tightened and she looked away. "So, my bad."

It stung, but he knew he'd given her good reason.

He didn't need his mother to be around to be disappointed in him.

He was disappointed in him all by himself.

"Just because things have turned out the way they have doesn't mean I won't hold up my end of the bargain," he finished gruffly.

She went white. "I knew you'd get bored with me quickly, but that really *was* fast."

"Bored!" The word nearly choked him. "God in heaven, Deanna, where the hell'd you get that idea?"

Her arms crossed over her chest. Her ghostly white coloring was being rapidly replaced by a flush. "You obviously can't wait to get rid of me."

"You're the one who's packing up, sweetheart, remember?" He shoved the suitcase so hard it slid off the bed and crashed crookedly onto the floor.

The latches sprang open and her clothing spilled out.

"Now look what you've done!"

"I'm not bored with you," he said flatly. He had plenty of emotions where she was concerned. Emotions he hadn't wanted to face, but not a one of them was boredom. "If you want to leave, I've got no reason to make you stay. My father is gone. There's no sign of foul play. No sign of anything. He's gone." The words tasted bitter and he had to stop. Clear his throat. "Either he chose to go and doesn't want to come back, not for Lily or any of the rest of us, or he's dead."

And despite the tension between them—tension he knew that he alone was responsible for creating—her expression softened. "Drew. I wish you wouldn't think that way."

"There's hope, and then there's holding on to a fantasy."

She looked pained. "And fantasies can't live forever, can they?" She slid past him and crouched in front of her suitcase, flattening it out on the floor. The thin strappy shirt thing that she wore to sleep in slid out along with a pair of lacy panties, and she tossed both back inside. "It *has* been only a few weeks. If your father is injured somewhere—"

"—we would have heard by now." He hated the words even as he said them because there was still a part of him that wanted to believe otherwise. It was the same part that had wanted to believe the cancer treatments would save his mother.

"And with Dad gone, there's no need for you to go through with this marriage business. I'll still pay what we agreed," he assured doggedly. "The bank'll be open Monday. I'll have the money wired into your account as soon as I can arrange it."

She snatched up the pink dress again and balled it up. "I know I can thank you for prodding my mother into counseling because she never would have done so because of me, though you could have told me yourself that you'd talked with her behind my back. But I don't *want* your money." Her voice had turned chilly. She pitched the dress into the suitcase. "I never did."

The back she presented to him might as well have been a gauntlet tossed down in challenge and he spun her around on her knees, grabbing her hand. He pushed his thumb against the diamond ring that she still wore, despite everything. "I didn't intentionally do anything behind your back. And the money's why you agreed to all this."

She snatched her arm away. "I agreed because you asked for my help."

He winced. "And because you needed my

help with your mother's debt," he insisted doggedly.

The look she gave him was almost pitying. "I'm not going to argue with you." In one sweeping armful, she'd shoved everything haphazardly back into the suitcase and flipped it closed. "If you want to believe I'm all about the Benjamins, then go ahead. At the moment I have more important things to do." She hit the latches for a second time.

"Like what?"

She pushed to her feet. "Like getting away from you," she snapped. "Isabella's already offered to drive me to San Antonio." Her lips twisted. "And don't worry. I told her the truth about us this morning. So *you* won't have to." She stepped around him, heading for the door, but not quickly enough for him to miss the tears in her eyes.

He shot up and blocked her way. "If it wasn't the money, then *why?*"

"Because I'm in love with you!" She shoved at his chest. "And now that we've got that out of the way, get out of my way so I can get out of yours."

He felt an ache in the center of his chest that had nothing to do with the surprising strength of her shove. "I don't want you out of my way," he admitted slowly.

"Of course you do," she said impatiently. "Nobody knows better than I do that the quickest route out of your life is to make the mistake of falling in love with you." Her voice went hoarse as she tried to slip around him to reach the door. "So I'm just going to make it easy on all of us and go home where I belong."

"Dammit, Deanna." His thoughts were clamoring inside his head as he caught her around the waist, hauling her up against him. "Would you stop for just one minute and listen?"

"Don't worry. I'm sure with a little effort you can find another assistant who'll be as foolishly agreeable as I've—"

He swore under his breath and shut off her words in the most effective way he could.

With his mouth.

She went rigid.

But he kept his mouth on hers. Until he felt the thin, tight line of her lips start to soften. Until he felt the fists pushing at his shoulders start to relax. Only then did he pull his lips from hers. "Where you belong is with me," he said quietly, and wondered why in the hell it had taken him so damn long to admit what his heart had been telling him.

"Is that so?" Her voice was still cool. But her mossy-green eyes had gone round.

"Yeah, that's so," he returned evenly. "And I know because where I belong is with you."

Her lips parted. She blinked rapidly, but her eyes grew even wetter. A diamond-bright tear clung perilously to her eyelashes before slowly falling to her cheek. "You don't mean that. You're just upset about your father."

"I am upset about my father," he agreed. "But if I let you walk out of that door, then I'm living up to every failure he's accused me of." He moved his unsteady hands to cup her face. "I've been so busy telling myself what you were to me that I missed *seeing* what you were to me." He caught the teardrop with his thumb. "But I'm not telling anymore." He drew in a hard breath. "I'm just…feeling," he finished roughly.

She stared at him. And even though more tears had joined the first, he could still see the uncertainty in her gaze.

Uncertainty that he'd caused.

And he realized even more just what real fear was.

It was losing what you loved most of all without ever having had a chance to show it.

"You said you loved me," he reminded, and his own eyes were suddenly burning.

Her throat worked. She looked away. Then looked up at him. Her eyes had gone to emerald. "I do. But that doesn't mean I have to always like you," she whispered.

His knees actually went weak. Maybe it was fear finally leaving him. Maybe it was relief.

But he knew in that moment that he would do everything in his power to never let this woman go.

She'd been his helper. His right hand. His conscience and his comfort. She was exactly what Drew's father had told Drew he'd needed to find.

His Molly.

And she'd been there in front of him all this time.

Drew's Deanna.

He pressed his lips to her forehead. Over her wet eyes. And finally, with more gentleness than he knew he was capable of, on her lips. "Tell me you'll never leave me."

Deanna sucked in a shuddering breath that tasted of hope and it was strong enough to dispel hopelessness. Her gaze searched Drew's.

And all she saw was *him*. The same man he'd always been. The charmer. The loner.

He hadn't pushed people away to keep them out, she realized with startling clarity. He'd done it to protect what was within. The boy whose first love had cheated on him. The man whose beloved mother was stolen by cancer. And now the man whose father had seemingly disappeared from the face of the earth.

She slowly reached up and laid her palm along his jaw. Her thumb slowly brushed over his cheek, smoothing away the trail of moisture that she'd never expected to see. Her heart stopped climbing up her throat and slowly, peacefully, settled back in her chest. Only this time, it was as wide-open as the heart that she could see in his eyes as he looked back at her.

"I loved you even before I knew I loved you," she whispered. She pushed up on her toes and pressed her lips to his. "And I will never leave you," she vowed.

His arms swept behind her back, nearly crushing her to him, he held her so tightly. But she didn't care. She was exactly where she wanted to be.

And she knew at last, with every fiber of her soul, that she was exactly where *he* wanted to be, too.

Epilogue

"Hey, old timer." The police officer stepped out of his cruiser and warily approached the bedraggled man slowly shuffling along the side of the highway. He'd gotten a call from a concerned citizen about a possible vagrant hitchhiking on the edge of town. "Where you heading?"

The man slowly turned to look at him. Even when the officer shone the beam of his flashlight over the wanderer, the man's thick hair was too matted with grime to tell the color. There were only a few things that were obvious to the officer.

One, the old man looked like he'd been to

hell and back. And the clothes that were in no better shape than the hair smelled like it, as well.

And two, the man's eyes were unfocused and vacant.

The officer sighed. The man reminded him of his own old man, when the Alzheimer's had been getting bad.

He stepped closer, keeping his voice easy. "You look like you could use a sandwich. Maybe a cup of coffee." He glanced back at his cruiser and wished that he hadn't turned on the beacon. He didn't want the flashing lights spooking the guy. "If you're on your way somewhere, I can give you a lift." *Straight to a hospital,* he thought.

He glanced back at the old man, surprised to see that he'd begun shuffling his way again along the highway. He looked dead set on leaving behind the last few lights of town, heading on down the dark road. "Hold on there." He caught up to the wanderer, wrapping his arm around the guy's arm. He felt sturdier than the officer expected, but this time he was prepared. When the wanderer tried to shove him off, he held fast. "We're going to get you some help. It'll be warm. And safe."

The man looked annoyed. "Leave me alone.

I'm in a hurry." Despite his appearance and his dazed expression, his voice was strong. He looked up suddenly at the sky, his vacant eyes narrowing.

The officer glanced up, too, but all he saw were the blinking lights of a jet high in the sky. He looked back at the man. "I can help you get where you're going if I know where you're heading. Home?"

The man pushed at the officer's hands. "Not home. The baby. I've gotta find the baby."

The officer slowly tightened his grip. The wanderer was easily as tall as he was, but there'd still be no match between them. He began steering the guy toward the cruiser. "Sure," he soothed. The guy definitely needed medical attention. "We'll find the baby."

High above the highway, Deanna sprawled on one of the well-cushioned couches inside the private jet that Drew had somehow managed to procure nearly out of thin air. She still felt breathless from the way he'd rushed her out to the airfield and onto the plane.

She felt even more breathless considering his arms were presently looped around her.

She slowly ran her palms down his forearms, loving the feel of the slightly rough hair against her palms. "We could have waited until morning to return to San Diego," she told him, not for the first time. Her palms reached his hands and her heart jiggled around when his hands turned so that his palms met hers.

"We're not heading to San Diego."

She sat upright, and looked over her shoulder at him. "But I thought—"

"I know what you thought." He threaded his fingers through her hair, slowly tucking it behind one ear. "But even the best assistant in the world doesn't know what the boss is thinking every minute of the day."

She made a point of looking at her watch. "It's actually the night," she pointed out drily. Midnight, in fact. And she recognized all too well the glint in his eyes. It was the glint that warned her Drew Fortune was up to something. Something probably brilliant, but still… something. "If we're not going to back to San Diego, then where?" She supposed Los Angeles wasn't out of the question. The headquarters of Fortune Forecasting *was* located there, and by default, both offices had been under his authority since his father disappeared.

"All in due time, Dee." He tugged her back against him and his lips pressed against the curve of her neck.

Heat streaked through her. They were completely alone in the cabin of the jet. The flight crew, comprised only of the pilot and copilot, were closed behind the cockpit door. Still, she wasn't entirely sure how she felt when Drew's hands began working their way beneath the hem of her sweater.

But then his hands reached her breasts and she let out a long, shaking breath as his fingers nimbly traced over the lace cups of her bra.

Who was she kidding?

When Drew touched her, she couldn't think of anything but *more.* More of him touching her. More of her touching him.

"That night in the barn was incredible," he murmured, still dropping kisses along her neck. "You were incredible."

Deanna's mouth went dry. Her fingers tightened around his forearms. "So were you." She sucked in a breath when he tugged the cups of her bra aside and his fingers closed around her bare flesh. She felt suddenly steeped in desire.

He shifted slightly and instead of sitting half reclined on the couch, she found herself lying on it with Drew leaning over her. His brown gaze looked like melted chocolate as it roved over her face. "There was just one problem."

She curved her hands over his shoulders,

trying to tug him back down to her. But he didn't move. So she levered herself up until her lips reached his. "What was that?"

"No light."

Her entire body flushed. "I...didn't mind." Which had to have been obvious.

He laughed softly. "I didn't mind, either. But even while you were turning me inside out with the way you were seducing me—"

"—seducing *you!*"

"I couldn't help thinking about making love to you like that all over again, with every single light blazing."

Now her insides felt like melted chocolate.

She glanced again at the closed door to the cockpit. The cabin was by no means brightly lit, but it was also not in the least bit shadowy. And the couch *was* inviting...

His eyes darkened. "I really love the way you think," he murmured, and slowly pressed his mouth to hers, kissing her so deeply that colors began exploding inside her head. "But not here," he said huskily when he finally did lift his head.

She just looked at him, uncomprehending. "What?"

"Not here," he murmured, dropping another much more chaste kiss on her lips. "First we need this." He worked a hand between them and her adrenaline shot up a few thousand notches.

But he didn't do anything but pull his hand out from between them a moment later.

And when he lifted himself off her altogether and moved off the couch, she frowned, reaching out her arms for him again. "Where are you going?"

"Not far from you." He smiled faintly. "That's a promise." He closed his hands around hers and only then did she realize he was holding something else besides her. "This is what I realize we need." He nudged her ring finger and she stared in shock at the two platinum wedding bands that he slipped over the tip of her finger. The metal felt warm from having been in his pocket.

Hardly daring to breath, she looked from the matching rings to his face. "Drew?"

"Turns out, I find myself in need of a wife." His expression was uncommonly uncertain as he knelt beside the couch.

"You don't say." Her voice was faint. Probably because her heart had lodged itself several inches above where it belonged.

"I do." The corner of his lips kicked up,

making her heart swell a little more. "But I also know that not just anyone will do."

She swallowed, incapable at that moment of a response.

His voice dropped a notch. "It takes a specialized person to make the terms of some deals come together just right." He slipped the two wedding bands off the tip of her finger, and then held the smaller, narrower of the two up between them.

His hand was shaking.

She didn't even try to stop the moisture collecting behind her eyes from spilling over. "What kind of terms?"

"Nonnegotiable, I'm afraid." He cleared his throat softly. "As long as we both shall live."

Her heart seemed to leave her chest altogether. Pure joy was suddenly the organ that pumped blood through her veins. "I think that is acceptable."

His gaze met hers. "Are you sure, Deanna?"

She lifted the larger, wider ring out of his hand and held it up between them.

Her hand was shaking.

"Nonnegotiable," she said softly. "I will laugh with you. I will cry with you. And as long as I have breath in my body, I will love you. Is that agreeable to you?"

"More than." His voice sounded raw. "Too bad my father won't be around to see what he brought about."

She leaned into him and slowly pressed a kiss to his forehead. Then his lips. "Your father will see. On this earth or not, he'll see."

He was silent for a moment. "I don't know if I believe that."

"Then I'll believe it enough for both of us," she whispered, "until you do."

His gaze met hers and she knew she was looking into the eyes of a man who knew what it was to love deeply.

To love *her*.

"Will you marry me, Deanna?"

Tears slid down her cheeks. "Yes, please."

His lips slanted. "We'll put this in place, then, until we get it done officially in a few hours." He slowly slid the wedding band onto her ring finger where it fit perfectly against her beautiful diamond.

"Okay." Her voice was faint as she pushed his ring onto the hand he held out for her, too.

She had to take a moment just to revel in the breathtaking sight of a wedding band—from her—on his bronzed finger. It was almost unbearably sexy.

Then his words belatedly sank in. "A few *hours?*"

"Flight plan is Las Vegas. I have it all planned out." He lifted her hand and kissed her finger over the rings, then pressed her palm flat against his chest where she could feel the heavy throb of his heartbeat. "Unless you really do want a wedding with all the frills." He grimaced a little, still Drew, no matter what. "I suppose for a short while, I can wait."

She started smiling and wondered if she would ever stop. "Well, good for you," she murmured and she slipped her hand behind his neck and slowly drew him to her. "But I can't wait."

And a few hours later when their plane landed in Las Vegas, they didn't.

* * * * *

Get 4 FREE REWARDS!

We'll send you 2 FREE Books plus 2 FREE Mystery Gifts.

Harlequin® Romance Larger-Print books feature uplifting escapes that will warm your heart with the ultimate feel-good tales.

FREE Value Over **$20**

YES! Please send me 2 FREE Harlequin® Romance Larger-Print novels and my 2 FREE gifts (gifts are worth about $10 retail). After receiving them, if I don't wish to receive any more books, I can return the shipping statement marked "cancel." If I don't cancel, I will receive 4 brand-new novels every month and be billed just $5.34 per book in the U.S. or $5.74 per book in Canada. That's a savings of at least 15% off the cover price! It's quite a bargain! Shipping and handling is just 50¢ per book in the U.S. and 75¢ per book in Canada.* I understand that accepting the 2 free books and gifts places me under no obligation to buy anything. I can always return a shipment and cancel at any time. The free books and gifts are mine to keep no matter what I decide.

119/319 HDN GMYY

Name (please print)

Address _____ Apt. #

City _____ State/Province _____ Zip/Postal Code

Mail to the **Reader Service:**
IN U.S.A.: P.O. Box 1341, Buffalo, NY 14240-8531
IN CANADA: P.O. Box 603, Fort Erie, Ontario L2A 5X3

Want to try 2 free books from another series? Call 1-800-873-8635 or visit www.ReaderService.com.

Get 4 FREE REWARDS!

We'll send you 2 FREE Books plus 2 FREE Mystery Gifts.

FREE Value Over **$20**

Both the **Romance** and **Suspense** collections feature compelling novels written by many of today's best-selling authors.

Get 4 FREE REWARDS!

We'll send you 2 FREE Books plus 2 FREE Mystery Gifts.

Harlequin® Heartwarming™ Larger-Print books feature traditional values of home, family, community and—most of all—love.

FREE Value Over $20

READERSERVICE.COM

Manage your account online!

- Review your order history
- Manage your payments
- Update your address

> ### We've designed the Reader Service website just for you.

Enjoy all the features!

- Discover new series available to you, and read excerpts from any series.
- Respond to mailings and special monthly offers.
- Browse the Bonus Bucks catalog and online-only exculsives.
- Share your feedback.

Visit us at:

ReaderService.com